THE
MILLS & BOON®
Centenary Collection

**Celebrating 100 years of romance with
the very best of Mills & Boon**

D1381785

First published in Great Britain 2008
by Harlequin Mills & Boon Limited,
Eton House, 18-24 Paradise Road, Richmond, Surrey TW9 1SR

ISBN: 978 0 263 86622 3

77-1108

Harlequin Mills & Boon policy is to use papers that are
natural, renewable and recyclable products and made from
wood grown in sustainable forests. The logging and
manufacturing processes conform to the legal environmental
regulations of the country of origin.

Printed and bound in Spain
by Litografia Rosés S.A., Barcelona

A Sicilian Marriage

by

Michelle Reid

MILLS & BOON

Pure reading pleasure

Michelle Reid grew up on the southern edges of Manchester, the youngest in a family of five lively children. But now she lives in the beautiful county of Cheshire with her busy executive husband and two grown-up daughters. She loves reading, the ballet, and playing tennis when she gets the chance. She hates cooking, cleaning, and despises ironing! Sleep she can do without and produces some of her best written work during the early hours of the morning.

CHAPTER ONE

NINA did not want to listen to this. In fact she was so sure she didn't that if she hadn't been sitting in her own home she would have seriously contemplated getting up from the lunch table and walking out.

As it was, all she could do was stare glassy-eyed at her mother and silently wish her a million miles away.

'Don't look at me like that,' Louisa said impatiently. 'You may like to think that the state of your marriage is none of my business, but when it is I who has to listen to ugly speculation and gossip about it then it becomes my business!'

'Does it?' Her daughter's cool tone said otherwise. 'I don't recall ever questioning you about the many reports on your various lovers throughout the years.'

Her mother's narrow shoulders tensed inside the fitted white jacket she was wearing, which did so much for her fabulous dark looks. At fifty-one years old, Louisa St James could still pass for thirty. Born in Sicily, the youngest of five Guardino children, Louisa had taken the lion's share in the beauty stakes, along with her twin sister Lucia. As small girls they'd wowed everyone with their black-haired, black-eyed enchantment, and when they'd grown into stunning young women besotted young men had beaten paths to the Guardino door. Now in her middle years, and with her twin sadly gone, Louisa could still grab male attention like a magnet. But a lifetime spent being admired had made Louisa so very conceited that Nina could sometimes see by her expression that she was bewildered as to how her womb had dared to produce a child that bore no resemblance to her at all.

Nina was tall and fair, and quiet and introverted. She looked out on the world through her English father's cool blue eyes, and when trouble loomed she locked herself away behind a wall of ice where no one could reach her. In her mother's Sicilian eyes the burning fires of all the passions were alien to her daughter, and she tended to treat Nina as if she did not know what they were.

'Your father made me a widow ten years ago, which means I am allowed to take as many lovers as I choose without raising eyebrows,' Louisa defended, completely ignoring the way she'd been taking lovers for most of Nina's life. 'Whereas your marriage is barely out of the honeymoon stage and already gossip about it is hot!'

Hot? Nina almost choked on the word, because the last thing she would have called her marriage was—*hot*. Cold, more like. A soulless waste of space. A mistake so huge it should be logged as an official disaster!

'If it's just gossip you're concerned about then you're talking to the wrong person,' she responded. 'Rafael is your culprit—go and talk to him.'

With that she got up, not quite finding the courage to walk out of the room but doing the next best thing by going to stand in front of the closed glass doors that led out onto the terrace.

Behind her the thin silence feathered her slender backbone. Her cold indifference to whatever her husband was doing had managed to shock her mother into stillness—for a moment or two.

'You are a fool, Nina,' she then announced bluntly.

Oh, yes, Nina agreed, and she stared out towards the glistening blue waters of the Mediterranean and wished she was on the little sailboat she could see gliding across the calm crystal sea.

'Because it is not only gossip. I saw them together for myself, *cara* and even a blind woman could not mistake the chemistry they were generating it was so—'

Hot, Nina supplied the word because it seemed much more suitable now than it had earlier.

Her mother used a sigh. 'You should keep him on a much tighter leash,' she went on. 'The man is just too gorgeous and sexy to be left to his own devices—and you know what he's like! Women fall over themselves to get closer to him, and he doesn't bother to push them away. He could charm a nun out of her chastity if he put his mind to it, yet how often are you seen at his side? Instead of isolating yourself up here on your hilltop you should be out there with him, making your presence felt—then *she* would not be trying to get her claws back into him and *I* would not be sitting here having to tell you things that no mother wants to—'

'Where?' Nina inserted.

'Hmm?'

Turning around, Nina was in time to watch her mother blink her lovely long black eyelashes, having lost the main plot of her exposé because she'd been so much more comfortable lecturing her daughter on things she knew very little about.

'Where did you see them?' She extended her question.

'Oh.' Understanding returned, sending those slender shoulders into an unhappy shrug. 'In London, of course…'

Of course, Nina echoed—London being the place Rafael spent most of his time these days, which was pretty ironic when she was the Londoner and he was the Sicilian.

'I was eating out with friends when I spotted them across the restaurant. Someone's mobile was ringing. When it just kept on, I looked up, and that is when I saw them. I was so shocked at first I just stared! I watched him pick his ringing cellphone up off the table, and without taking his eyes off her face he switched it off and put it in his pocket!' Louisa took a tight breath. 'I had this horrible feeling that it was you calling him, so to watch him do that made me—'

'It wasn't me,' Nina said, though she had a good idea who the caller had been.

'I am so relieved to hear you say that. I cannot tell you how it felt to think that you might need him and he—'

'Did they see you?' she cut in.

Her mother's smile was dry, to say the least. 'Darling, they were being so intense across that candlelit table for two that they didn't see anyone,' she said. 'I thought about going over there to confront them—but, well… It was just a bit embarrassing to witness my son-in-law getting it on with my niece in public.'

'So you left them to it?'

'It could have been innocent.'

But it wasn't, Nina thought—and how did she know that? Because this particular woman was more than *just* her mother's niece.

'And that is not all of it,' Louisa pushed on. 'I saw them again later on, going—going into your apartment building.'

'How unfortunate for them,' Nina drawled. 'Did you follow them there, by any chance?'

Dark eyes gave a flash of defiance. 'Yes, if you must know. I did not like what I was seeing, so I thought I would keep an eye on them! *She* should not even be in London,' she tagged on stiffly. 'New York is her hunting ground, and it would have been better for all of us if she'd just stayed there.'

'So you spied on them going into our apartment building…?' Nina prompted.

Louisa looked pained suddenly. 'I could see them through the glass doors, Nina! They were standing there, waiting for the lift to come. He—he was touching her face while she gazed up at him. It was all so…'

Oh, my… Nina thought, and had to turn away again so that her mother wouldn't see what was happening to her face.

Another thick silence crawled around them while her mother brooded over what she'd said and Nina stared at the view. The little sailboat had gone, she saw, disappearing round the headland to her right, where the ancient city of Syracuse clustered around the tiny island of Ortigia.

When her gaze drifted to the left she could just make

out Mount Etna in the distance, shrouded in one of her hazy mists. The volcano had been very active lately, spewing out the most spectacular paratactic displays throughout the long hot summer. Now winter was here, and although the days were quite warm for December, the gentle plume of smoke she could see rising from Etna's peak said the volcano had cooled her ardour to suit the cooler temperature—for now, at least.

'How does she look?' she asked after a minute.

'The same,' came the flat reply. 'As beautiful as ever, if not—' *More so*, was the observation left hanging in the air. 'She reminded me of her mother,' Louisa added huskily.

Nina smiled a bleak little smile. The beautiful dark-haired Lucia had produced a beautiful dark-haired daughter and oh, how Louisa had always envied her twin for doing that.

'What are you going to do?' her mother asked after another of those heavy silences.

Do—? Nina turned to face the room again, wearing a smile that was so paper-dry it actually hurt her lips as they stretched. 'Rafael paid a high price for my loyalty and he'll have it, whatever *he* decides to do. I've already told you that you're talking to the wrong person about this.'

'Oh Nina…' The pained sigh matched her mother's expression as she watched Nina cross back to the table. 'How did you and Rafael ever get yourselves into this state?'

'Money, darling,' Nina drawled in her very best boarding school English as she sat down again. 'Our appalling lack of it and his abominable excess.'

'Rubbish,' Louisa dismissed. 'You adored each other. Rafael was besotted with you from the first moment he looked at you, and you were so in love with him that even that—that prissy manner your father insisted on breeding into you used to melt for him.'

A game, Nina cynically named that little deception. It had all been just a very clever game they'd played out for the sake of anyone who happened to be interested. Rafael had set the rules by which their marriage would run and Nina had agreed to keep to them—for a price. They were to show a loving front to the world, and in return he would keep the great Guardino name clear of bankruptcy.

Some price for him to pay for what had only been a face-saving exercise, Nina conceded, recalling just how much it had cost him to bail her grandfather out. But then saving face had always been of paramount importance to Rafael. The monumental size of his pride demanded it.

That and some deeply hidden hang-ups he never spoke about but which ruled his life far more than he realised.

'It was the sole reason why she went away in the first place,' Louisa insisted. 'Once she realised what was happening between the two of you she really had no other option but to step back and leave the field clear.'

And there, Nina thought, was *the* deception. 'Yes,' she agreed.

Rafael had been hovering on the brink of asking her beautiful cousin to marry him when Marisia had discovered something about him she couldn't accept and walked out. She'd walked out on his love, his fabulous wealth and, most important of all, she'd walked all over his precious pride as she went.

'You used to be so happy together.'

'Delirious.'

'Rafael used to eat you with his eyes and he did not care who saw him doing it.'

Nina found a wry smile for that observation—wry because in an odd way her mother was right. Rafael *had* eaten her with his eyes.

With his eyes, his lips, his tongue, his…

But that had only been for the first few wild months of their marriage, when they'd set out to fool the world and had done it so successfully that they'd actually managed to fool themselves at the same time.

And the special ingredient to aid and abet this deception?

Sex. She named it grimly. They'd been so bowled over by the discovery of a wildly passionate and very mutual sexual attraction to each other that it had shocked them stupid for a time. Blinded them to the reality of what they really felt for each other.

Blinded her anyway, Nina amended as something worryingly close to despair began to swell up inside her. Blinded her enough to let her believe that they were actually in love.

Love. She could scoff at the very word now. As far as Rafael was concerned he had simply played the game, as any man would play the game, and taken what was on offer because it had been there to take, whereas she…

Well, blinded as she had been, she had committed the ultimate sin in his eyes, by taking their relationship one step further—unwittingly crossing into forbidden territory—and in doing so had forced Rafael to open her eyes to the size of her mistake.

Since then—nothing.

Nothing, she repeated, feeling the desolation of that nothing echoing in the deep, dark void of her now empty heart.

Louisa must have seen it, because she reached across the table to cover one of Nina's hands. 'I know you have been through a bad time recently, darling,' she murmured very gently. 'God knows, we all suffered the loss with you, believe me…'

Nina stared at their two hands, resting against pristine white linen, and wished her mother would just shut up.

'Your grandfather still blames himself.'

'It was no one's fault.' Her reply was quiet and stilted, her thoughts even more so—cold and bleak.

'Have you told him that?'

'Of course I have. Countless times.'

'Have you told Rafael the same thing…?'

Suddenly she wanted to run from the room again. 'What is this?' She sighed. 'An inquisition?'

'He worries me—*you* worry me— No, don't get angry…' Louisa begged as Nina reclaimed her hand and shot back to her feet. Louisa stood too, her tone suddenly anxious. 'It's been six months since you lost the baby…'

Six months, two weeks and eight hours, to be precise, Nina thought.

'Before that the two of you were never seen apart and now you are never seen together! You just shut everyone out, Nina—Rafael more than anyone! And—OK,' Louisa said, 'I understand that you needed time to recover, but after what I've just told you, surely you must see that it is time for you to put that tragic loss

aside if you don't want your marriage to end in trag-
edy too!'

For an answer Nina spun on her heels and walked
away, hating everything—everyone—and despising
herself. She didn't want to think about her poor lost
baby; she didn't want to think about Rafael!

Her heart ached, her bones ached. She caught a
glimpse of herself reflected in the mirror hanging on the
wall and was shocked into stillness by what she saw.
Her skin was pale by nature, but it had now taken on
the consistency of paste. Her eyes looked bruised, her
mouth small and tight. Tension was gnawing at the fine
layer of flesh covering her cheekbones, making her
look gaunt and wretched—and she was not going to
cry! she told herself furiously. She just was not going—

'He is not a man to neglect like this, *cara*,' her mother
persisted. '*She* wants him back. And you have just got
to face it!'

I won't faint if you say her name, you know,' she
drawled.

It was like a red rag to a bull. Her mother's response
was incensed. 'Sometimes I find it difficult to believe that
you're my child at all! Do you have *any* of my Sicilian
blood? Marisia—yes—that is her name, and you did not
faint! Your cousin *Marisia* was in love with your husband
long before you came on the scene, and by the way she
is behaving I would say that she is still in love with
him—yet you stand here looking as if you could not
care less that they are conducting a very public affair!'

'So you want me to do—what?' Nina swung round,
blue eyes offering up their first flash of real emotion
since this whole horrible scene began. 'Am I supposed

to jump on the next flight to London and face them with what you've told me? Then what?' she challenged, moving back to the table to glare at her mother across it. 'You tell me, Mamma, how my half-Sicilian blood is supposed to respond once I've dragged it all out in the open—do I draw out my dagger and plunge it into both their chests with true Sicilian vendetta passion?'

'Now you are being fanciful just to annoy me,' Louisa said crossly. 'But, having asked me the question—*si*!' she retorted. 'Some drama from you would be a lot healthier than looking as if you don't give a damn!'

CHAPTER TWO

MAYBE I don't give a damn, Nina thought later, when she was alone in her bedroom. She didn't know if she cared one way or another what Rafael was doing.

And that was her problem—not knowing how she felt about anything.

A sigh slipped from her. Her mother's final volley before she'd left in a huff was still ringing in her ears.

'I suppose you will manage to drag yourself down from the hilltop to be present at your grandfather's birthday party tonight?'

Her weary, 'Of course I'll be there,' had made Louisa's lovely mouth pinch.

'There is no *of course* about it. You are in danger of becoming a hermit, Nina. For goodness' sake, snap out of it!'

'I had lunch three days ago in Syracuse with Fredo,' she'd retaliated. 'Hermits don't do that!'

'Hmph.' Louisa hadn't been impressed. 'That man is about as much use to you as the plethora of kind words and sympathy he will have dished out. You need to be pulled out of it, not encouraged to sink further in your wretched misery!'

Stopping what she was doing, Nina stood for a moment, blue eyes lost in a bleak little world of their own. Inside she could feel her heart beating normally. She breathed when she needed to and blinked her eyes. Her brain was functioning, feeding in information, and she was able to get information out, but when it came to her emotions, everything was just blank—nothing there, nothing happening. It was like living in a vacuum, with a defence space around her as big as a field.

'Oh, what's happened to me?' she breathed, looking around at the bedroom she'd used to share but now had to herself. Even in here the only sign that life was still going on was the black dress hanging up, which she was going to wear tonight.

Snap out of it, her mother had said, and Nina truly agreed with her. But—into what?

The sound of a car coming up the driveway stopped her thoughts and sent her over to the bedroom window. The prospect of yet another unexpected visitor dragged a groan from her throat that was cut short when she recognised the sleek, dark limousine.

It was Rafael.

Her heart gave a sudden tight little flutter—not with pleasure, but with a sinking sense of dismay. He wasn't due back from London for days, so what had brought him back here sooner than he'd intended?

Had someone told him about her mother's visit? Could he know what that visit had been about?

No, don't be stupid, she told the second sharp flutter that now had her freezing to the spot. He might be equipped to throw power around like thunderbolts, but even Rafael couldn't get from London to Sicily in the space of two short hours.

The car slowed to take a sweep around the circular courtyard, then came to a stop at the bottom of the shallow steps that led up to the house. Rafael didn't wait for Gino, his personal bodyguard and chauffeur, to climb out and open his door for him. With a brisk impatience that was his nature he pushed open the door and uncoiled his long frame from the back of the car. The top of his dark head caught the light from a golden sunset, then slid down to enrich the warm olive skin of his face as he paused to look at the house.

He was tall, he was dark, he was arrestingly handsome—a perfect example of a man in his prime. Black hair, golden skin, hard, chiselled features, straight, thin nose, and a firm and unsmiling and yet deeply, deeply sensual mouth.

Nina traced each detail as she stood there, despising herself for doing it yet unable to stop. Everything about him was so physically striking—the way he looked, the way he moved, the way he frowned with a restless impatience that was inherent in him. His dark silk suit was a statement in design architecture, tailored to a body built to carry clothes well—the wide shoulders, long arms and legs made up of steely muscle, wide chest and tight torso behind a white shirt.

But the really important things about Rafael had nothing to do with his physical appearance. He was frighteningly intelligent, razor-sharp, and ruthless to the core. The kind of man who had come from nothing and made himself into something in spite of all the odds stacked against him, amassing his wealth with a gritty determination that came from his fear of having nothing—again.

He was, Nina thought as she watched him turn to speak to Gino, a very suave, very sophisticated— mongrel. And she used the word quite deliberately. Rafael did not know where he had come from, so he'd spent most of his adult life hiding what he feared he might be by surrounding himself with status symbols of the kind of person he wanted to be.

Rejected by his mother before she had even bothered to register his birth, he had lived his childhood in a Sicilian state orphanage. The only thing that faceless creature had given him to cling to when she'd dumped his helpless newly born body on some unsuspecting stranger's doorstep had been a note pinned to the blanket he had been wrapped in.

'His name is Rafael,' the note had said, and he had gone through the latter stages of his childhood fighting to hell and back for the right to use that name.

The orphanage had called him Marco Smith, or Jones, or some Sicilian equivalent. For the first ten years of his life he had truly believed it to be his name, until the day something—an inbuilt instinct to be *someone*, probably—had sent him sneaking into the principal's office to steal a look at his personal file.

From that day on he had answered only to Rafael. Sheer guts and determination had brought him fighting and clawing to the age of sixteen, with his name legally changed to Rafael Monteleone—the Monteleone stolen from the man on whose doorstep he had been dumped.

But tenacity should be Rafael's middle name—or the one Nina would add in if she could. From the minute he'd left state care he had set out like a man with a single mission in life—which was to trace the mother who had abandoned him.

To finance his search he'd worked hard and long at anything, and for anyone who had paid a fair wage, until he had accumulated enough money to risk some of it on a little speculation—thereby discovering his true mission in life: to make money—pots of it—bank vaults of it—Etna-sized mountains of it in fact.

Strangely, though, as the money mountain had grown so his need to know his roots had diminished. Rafael had succeeded in becoming his own man. If you did not count some deeply buried fears that lurked beneath the surface of his iron-hard shell, which forced him to struggle with the most incredible inferiority complex.

'The mongrel syndrome'. Rafael's term, not Nina's. 'I could come from the loins of anything.'

Rafael lived with the awful fear that the blood running in his veins might be rotten. It didn't seem to help that the man he had built himself to be was so morally upright, honest and true that any suspicion of him being rotten inside was actually laughable. He could never know that for sure, so he dared not let his guard on himself drop for a moment—just in case something dreadful crept out.

How did Nina know all of this? The man himself had told her, during one of those long rare nights when they lay still closely entwined after the kind of loving that had always seemed to blend them into one. They'd swapped secret hopes and fears in the darkness because it had seemed so right, sharing—sharing everything. Bed to bodies, souls to minds.

That was the same night that she'd foolishly let herself believe he loved her, Nina recalled. To hear that soft, deep, slightly rasping voice reveal all its darkest secrets had, to her at least, been confirmation of something very special growing between them. She had discovered later that it was just another aspect of his complicated make-up that Rafael could bare his soul to her whilst keeping his heart well and truly shut.

It wasn't long after that night when she'd discovered they were going to have a baby. She'd been ecstatic; to her way of thinking a child of their very own would only bond them closer together. What it had actually done was drive them wide apart. And she would never forgive him for the brutality he had used in forming that gulf.

They had barely communicated since. From that moment on their lives had reverted to the original plan—she being the beautiful well-bred trophy wife Rafael had bought to shore up his bruised ego, and he the man she had sold herself to so he could keep her family in the luxury they were used to.

The only blot on this otherwise squeaky-clean landscape Rafael had made for himself was Marisia—his first-choice bride. The Guardino granddaughter with the pure Sicilian pedigree who'd walked out on him the moment she'd discovered his mongrel beginnings, leaving his pride in tatters at his feet.

'I will not marry a man who can't say who his mother is, never mind his father!' Marisia's harsh words to Nina echoed through the years. 'If you are so concerned about his feelings then you marry him. Trust me, *cara*, he will take you—just to leech onto your half-Guardino blood.'

He had done too—taken her—and it was pretty lowering to remember how eagerly she'd jumped at the chance. But then, she'd already been in love with him, though thankfully no one else knew that—including Rafael. He'd put his case in practical business terms, pointing out the financial advantages in marrying him and, because he was ruthless enough to use any persuasion, he had made her aware of other advantages by more physical means.

Oh, where had her pride been—her self-respect? How was it that she'd only had to look into his eyes to convince herself that she could see something burning there that made her cling to hope?

The sound of his laughter floated up to the window. Looking down, she saw his mouth had stretched into a grin. He had not done much of that recently, she mused.

Was that Marisia's doing? Had her cousin put the laughter back into Rafael?

Were they sleeping together?

Had it gone that far?

Did she care?

Nina turned away from the window, tense fingers coiling around her upper arms to bite hard. She wasn't ready to answer that question. She wasn't ready to face Rafael.

Oh, why did he have to come back here today of all days, when she needed time to think—to *feel* something, for God's sake?

The moment Rafael Monteleone stepped through the front door he felt the lingering residue of laughter he'd just shared with Gino die from his lips as a chill washed right over him.

It was the chill of cold silence.

He paused to stare at the perfectly symmetrical black and white floor that spread out in front of him like a chequered ocean—flat, cold, and as uninviting as the black wrought-iron work forming the curving staircase and the pale blue paint that coloured the walls.

Home, he mused, and thought about sighing—only to tamp down on the urge. Instead tension grabbed at his shoulders, then slid up the back of his neck before linking like steel fingers beneath his chin. He employed an army of staff to help keep this miserable if aesthetically stunning house running smoothly, yet but for the sound of Gino moving the car round to the garages he could be entirely alone here.

The sigh escaped—because he allowed it—because he needed to ease away some of his tension before he went looking for his wife.

Wife, he repeated. There was yet another word that had become a term of mockery—within the privacy of his mind, at least. He did not mock Nina—did not mock her at all. He mocked only himself, for daring to use the word in reference to the ghost-like image of that once beautiful person which now haunted this house.

He knew exactly where she was, of course. He'd felt the chill of her regard via her bedroom window from the moment he had stepped out of the car. If he closed his eyes he could even picture her standing there, slender and still, observing his arrival through beautiful blue eyes turned to glass.

'Good afternoon, sir,'

Ah, a real human being, Rafael thought dryly, then had to laugh privately at that when he lifted his eyes to the ancient silver-haired pole-faced butler, who'd come with the house and all of its other soulless fixtures and fittings.

'Good afternoon, Parsons,' he returned, and felt himself grimace at the very English sound of his own voice.

But then, this house was English—a small piece of England placed upon Sicilian soil like a defiance. Nina's father had had it built as a summer home for his wife and daughter to use when they visited. When Richard St James had died, leaving his wife and daughter virtually penniless, they'd been forced to sell up their fourteen-thousand-acre family estate in Hampshire and come to live here, bringing their faithful butler with them. The house belonged to Nina now, left to her in her father's will, along with a trust fund aimed to ensure that she completed her education in England.

And if all of that did not add up to a man with an axe to grind on his beautiful Sicilian wife's faithless hide, then he could not read character as well as he'd thought.

'There are several telephone messages for you.' Parsons' smooth voice intruded. 'I placed them in your study. One, from a—lady, sounded particularly urgent...'

Ignoring the slight hesitation before the word *lady*, Rafael offered a nod of his head in acknowledgment to the rest, but made no move towards his study. Instead he turned and headed for the stairs. Urgent messages or not, he had a chore to do that must take precedence.

Knowing and respecting this small ritual, Parsons melted away as silently as he had arrived, leaving Rafael to make the journey up the curving staircase to the upper landing, and from there through an archway which would take him to the bedroom apartments of a house he had agreed to live in only to please his wife.

A mistake? Yes, it had been a mistake, one of many he had made with the beautiful Nina, and all of which he intended to rectify—soon.

On that grim thought he arrived outside the bedroom suite, paused for a moment to brace his shoulders inside the smooth cut of his dark silk jacket, then gripped the handle and opened the door.

He never knocked. He found it beneath his dignity to knock before entering what he still considered to be their bedroom, even though they had not shared it for months.

Serenity prevailed—that was his first observation as he stepped into the room, closing the door behind him. She was wearing a blue satin wrap that covered her from throat to ankle and she was sitting at her dressing table, quietly filing her nails. Her hair was up, scraped back into an unflattering ponytail, and her face looked paler than usual—though that could be a trick of the fading light.

When she turned her head to look at him he met with a wall of blue glass.

'Ciao,' he murmured, keeping his voice pleasant, even though pleasure was not what he was feeling inside.

'Oh, hello,' she returned, 'I wasn't expecting to see you today.' With that excruciatingly indifferent comment, the blue glass dropped away again.

Irritation snapping at the back of his clenched teeth, Rafael let the hit to his ego pass. He crossed the room to an antique writing desk on which sat a silver tray complete with crystal decanter and glasses. The ever-discreet Parsons had begun this small piece of thoughtfulness at the beginning of their marriage, when they'd used to spend more time in the bedroom than out of it, and had determinedly continued the habit though he must know that their marriage was now in tatters.

The decanter held his favourite cognac. Lifting off the smooth crystal stopper, he placed it aside, then turned to look at Nina.

'You?' he invited.

She gave a shake of her lowered head. 'No, thanks.'

It was like talking to a dead person. Turning back to the tray, he poured himself a small measure, took it with him over to the window, then unclenched his jaw and drank.

Ritual rules, he mused as he stared out at the deepening sunset. Give her a minute or two and she was going to find an excuse to get up and leave the room.

Only this time he was going to stop her. This time he was going to stop the rot taking place in this room by bringing her—screaming and kicking if necessary—out of hiding and into reality.

His stomach warmed as the cognac reached it, and somewhere else inside him a different sensation gathered pace. The call to battle. He had wrecked this beautiful creature once, and now it was time to put her back together again.

With a bit of luck she would give him a chance to fortify himself with brandy before battle commenced, he mused wryly, unaware that the subject of his thoughts was already struggling to stay where she was.

CHAPTER THREE

TIMING was everything, Nina was reminding herself as she sat there fighting the urge to get up and go.

It was part of the ritual Rafael had developed, aimed to hide the true sickness in their relationship from the servants. He always came directly to her room when he arrived home, and stayed long enough to consume a measure of cognac. He always asked her if she wanted to join him in a glass and she always refused. After a suitable length of time one of them—usually her— would make up an excuse to leave.

But today was different. Today he had come in here wearing the shadow of another woman's kiss on his lips, and there was no way she could sit here playing this the way it usually played out. She either said something, or left. It came down to those two options, she told herself tautly.

Rafael turned. 'Nina, we need to talk—'

'Sorry.' She stood up. 'I'm going for a shower.'

'Later,' he frowned. 'This is important. I want to—'

'So is my shower,' she cut in. 'Y-you should have warned me you were coming home, then I could have told you that I am out tonight.'

'Your grandfather's birthday—I know.' He nodded. 'That is what I want to talk to you about.'

Not Marisia? 'Why? What has he done now?' she asked, in the wary voice of one who knew her devious grandparent well.

'Nothing,' Rafael said. 'I have not heard from him in several weeks. He is not the reason why I—'

'Then he's up to something.' Nina cut in on him yet again. A sigh escaped her. 'I suppose I had better try and find out what so I can—'

'I would prefer that you didn't…'

Just the way he said that was enough to put her nerve-ends on edge. Her chin came up. 'What is that supposed to mean?' she demanded, finding herself suddenly in danger of almost—almost making contact with his eyes. She looked away again—quickly.

If he noticed her avoiding gesture he kept it to himself. 'It means,' he murmured levelly, 'that I already know what he's up to, so you don't need to get involved.'

'He's *my* grandfather, Rafael. I have a right to know what he's doing if it means—'

'Not when it involves money, you don't,' he responded. 'That is my territory.'

The implication in that certainly hit where it hurt. 'Then I won't,' she answered stiffly. 'Taking care of my family is why I married you, after all. Thank you for reminding me.'

'I did not mean it like that.' He uttered a short sigh. 'I simply meant that I am able to handle him better if you don't interfere!'

Well, there you go, Nina thought. You are an interfering wife, as well as a useless, faithless, traitorous one. Things are on the move—hence the reintroduction of Marisia into his life, she supposed.

'I did not come home early to fight with you over your grandfather. I have something I need to tell you before—'

Time to leave, she decided. 'Tell me later.' Spinning away, she began walking quickly towards the bathroom, her spine tingling out a mocking challenge to the cowardly way she was retreating from this.

'Take a very healthy piece of advice, *mi amore* and don't do it…'

It was the silken edge to his voice that brought her to a wary standstill, with her fingers already gripping the handle to the bathroom door. Past experience with that tone warned her to beware—because the silkier Rafael's voice became the more dangerous he became. If she dared to open this door now then he would not hesitate to react.

'OK.' She turned, slender shoulders pressing back against the door. 'Say what you have to say,' she invited.

He was still standing by the window, so his face was shadowed by the sunset coming from behind him. But she could see the tension in his jawline; could *feel* his anger and frustration reaching out to her across the width of the room.

He held it all in check—he *always* held it in check! It was part of what they had now—Rafael taking what she dished out to him because his guilty conscience demanded it of him, and she dishing it out because— She didn't want to finish that—did not want to think about them as a *them* at all!

He moved at last, taking a few short steps so he could put his glass back down on the tray. When he turned to look at her his face was no longer shadowed, but right there in full focus.

Nothing showed on those hard aquiline features— nothing. But she suddenly felt as if the sky had darkened and a loud thunderclap followed by a lightning strike was piercing directly into her.

It was the way of the man—a force to be reckoned with. Love him or hate him, it was impossible to look at him and pretend she didn't feel a thing. In fact she hated him—she was sure that she did—but he could still hold her transfixed.

He was going to come close; she could actually sense him making that decision. Her nerve-ends began to scream, her fingers and palms beginning to sweat where she'd flattened them against the door behind her as he took that first deliberate step. They didn't do close any more, so it had to be a conscious decision. And he might possess good looks any woman would die to stake her claim to—a body any woman would kill to experience—but as those long legs brought him ever closer she felt like a tortoise contracting into its shell.

He came to a halt a couple of feet away, the telltale scent of him invading her private space first. He was big and lean, and stood head and shoulders over her with all the power of a smothering black cloud.

She had to close her eyes. 'Don't touch me,' she whispered.

'Then don't challenge me to,' he threw back in husky response.

The husky voice hurt her heart somehow; she tugged

in an anxious breath. Her stomach muscles were coiling into agonising knots.

'Look at me,' he urged. Her eyelids remained closed over vulnerable blue eyes and he released a sigh. 'We cannot go on like this, you know,' he murmured grimly.

Yes, we can, Nina thought, feeling the sudden burn of tears at the back of her eyes. We can go on for ever like this. I *like* it like this!

'We have to move on. *You* have to move on.'

Her lashes flicked up. 'You want a divorce?'

The words were out before she could stop them. His response shook her to the core. His hands came up and slammed against the door at either side of her trembling shoulders, and even as a shocked gasp shot from her chest in a frightened flurry he was shifting his stance. The next thing she knew his lean face was exactly level with hers.

Eyes as dark as a deep, deep ocean clashed with her eyes. It was not supposed to happen. She *never* let herself make eye contact, and now she could not break away! Her throat had locked, with tiny breaths of panic fighting to escape and heaving at her breasts.

He didn't speak, didn't even move again, and still nothing of what he was thinking showed in those hard features as he held her trapped there like a mesmerised cat.

Was he sleeping with Marisia?

Did she care? *Did* she care?

Confusion ran like quick fire in a dizzying circle inside her head.

Ask him, she told herself. Tell him what you know and just get it over with! She parted her trembling lips.

He covered them. It was that quick—that shocking.

Her first response was to pull away from him. The second was to freeze. The third was to feel that kiss in so many places she had believed could no longer feel anything. Now an incandescence was sweeping over her in a tingling, shining shimmer of heat.

It was the shock, she told herself. She just had not expected him do this. They hadn't kissed in months— hadn't touched unless it was in the company of others, when keeping up appearances made it necessary.

Which was why she rarely went anywhere with him—why she was standing here now, feeling everything as if it were their first ever kiss.

The tip of his tongue made a slow pass over the tip of her tongue, and a shaken whimper lodged in her throat.

He did it again—and again. No! she cried inside when she felt herself tremble and begin to respond.

That first tiny tremor was all it took to bring the ordeal to an end. He lifted his dark head, studied her for a few wretched moments, then said smoothly, 'Go for your shower. We don't want to be late.'

Rafael turned away from the sight of her white-face and shaken composure, his eyes glittering angrily now that she could not see them doing it. She looked like some child's broken and discarded doll, left leaning against the door.

Had that been his intention when he'd started this? To break her up some more?

No, was the answer. But that had been before she'd looked so damn vulnerable when she asked him if he wanted a divorce.

The rest of that brandy called to him. He was crossing the room to where he had left his glass when a sound from behind told him she was beginning to pull herself together again.

'We?' she murmured shakily. 'Y-You said *we* don't w-want to be late. *You* aren't coming.'

'Are you saying I'm not invited?' He picked up the brandy glass, noticed that his fingers were shaking and grimaced.

'I don't want you there.'

Well, that was blunt and to the point, he thought, and grimaced again. 'I am sure your grandfather will be delighted to see me.'

'If this has something to do with whatever he's up to then I don't want you spoiling his birthday!'

'Still his fiercest champion, *cara*?' he mocked.

'Just leave him alone,' she said shakily.

'I will be coming with you tonight,' he repeated. 'Resign yourself to it while you take your shower.'

The quiet and level quality of his tone did it, as he had known that it would. He heard her stifled sigh of defeat and turned in time to watch her disappear into the bathroom on a whisper of blue satin and quivering frustration.

The door closed with a slam. Rafael winced, then allowed himself a thin smile. She had not slammed anything in a long time. Maybe the kissing tactic had not been such a bad one after all...

CHAPTER FOUR

THE plain black silk jersey dress still hung ready on its hanger. Nina sent it an indifferent glance as she passed it on her way to select underwear from her lingerie drawer.

Black was not a colour that particularly flattered her, but her grandfather thought it did. He claimed the colour added drama to what he insensitively called her insipidness.

Nonno was an insensitive brute all round, she mused as she slipped a sheer black silk teddy on over her lightly perfumed skin. It never occurred to him that his opinion might hurt someone who had spent most of her life feeling thoroughly outshone by her vibrant Sicilian cousin.

'I only tell it as it is,' was one of his favourite statements.

Still, she loved him, and he loved her in his own unique way. So what if he was a reckless rogue who thought nothing of throwing away a million he didn't have on some no-hope business opportunity? Or, worse, gambled it away in a single night playing backgammon with his friends? He had been her tower of strength when her father had died and her mother had been too wrapped up in playing the merry widow to notice that her fifteen-year-old daughter needed her support. If Rafael thought she was going to let him challenge the old man tonight of all nights, then—

Rafael…

Just thinking his name was enough to cause the tension knot in her stomach to tighten as she drew black silk stockings up her long, slender legs.

Was he sleeping with Marisia?

She had just spent the last hour in the bathroom trying to work out why she had not just come out with it and asked him that question.

A desire not to know, maybe because confirmation would mean she would have to face the answer, crucified dignity and all?

But—no, there was more to it than that. They might not have a real marriage any more, but she still found it difficult to believe Rafael would be unfaithful to his marriage vows—and where would it put his precious pride if he did let Marisia back into his life after what she'd done to him?

Now you're calling your own mother a liar, she thought. Are you that desperate to hang on to the status quo—useless, empty thing that it is?

She wished she could answer that question too, but she couldn't. Each time she approached it she met with a brick wall in her head.

Self-preservation. She'd been living with it as her best friend for months, so she recognised it when it threw up one of its walls.

Just stay there while I get through this evening, she begged it. Grandpa deserved that much consideration, even if it did mean enduring Rafael's company and all that role-playing togetherness.

That kiss had been…

Oh, don't go there. She groaned silently as her blood sped through her heart in an accelerated rush and her lips began to heat.

She was beginning to feel things, she realised starkly. Some walls might still be shooting up, but others were beginning to fall.

The black dress dropped into place over the teddy. Slipping her feet into high-heeled patent leather shoes, she turned to look at herself in the mirror and saw exactly what she had expected to see—a blonde with blue eyes and pink lips wearing a short black dinner dress. Nothing more, nothing less.

The dress relied on its expensive designer cut for its classic styling, and on her slender figure for the rest. She'd left her freshly washed and blow-dried hair to float around her shoulders and her make-up appeared to come down to only a flick of mascara to darken her eyelashes and a coating of lipstick. In reality, it had taken some careful work to disguise how pale and bruised she was really looking beneath.

With a flick of her fingers through her silk-fine hair, followed by a nervous smoothing of them down the sides of the dress, she turned to gather up her clutch purse from the bed and headed for the door, pausing long enough to heave in a deep, steadying breath.

I'll get through this, she told herself determinedly. Then opened the door and went out to face an evening which promised to be an ordeal.

She could hear Rafael talking in his study as she came down the stairs. The door was open, and her first glimpse of him showed a man in a dinner suit who was completely at ease with himself. Lean hips rested against the edge of the desk, long legs were stretched out and crossed, one hand lost in his jacket pocket while the other held his cellphone to his ear.

He looked up, the deep, Italian tones of his voice going silent as their gazes held for a few seconds like two guarded adversaries, trying to read the other's thoughts. She looked away first, and he returned to his conversation. As she continued down the stairs she noticed Parsons standing by the front door, with her black winter coat draped over his arm.

Her first warm smile of the day arrived as she crossed the black and white chequered floor towards him. 'Is it very cold out there?' she asked lightly.

'It is the price we pay for the clear blue skies we enjoyed today,' the butler replied. He was about to hold out the coat for her when Rafael stopped him.

'I'll do that.' The sound of his loose-limbed stride coming towards them lost Nina her smile. He came to a stop directly behind her.

'Of course, sir,' the ever-correct Parsons conceded, falling back a few discreet steps to stand ready to open the door.

Reaching round, Rafael took her purse from her. 'Transformed and on time,' he said lightly. 'You never fail to impress me, *mia cara.*'

With the urge to tense up tugging on muscles she had to fight to keep relaxed, Nina said nothing as she slid her arms into the coat sleeves. Silk-lined wool settled gently across her slender shoulders, and the light touch of his hands brought her round to face him. She stood staring at the front of his white dress shirt while he spent a few seconds releasing her hair from the coat's fake fur collar, then her purse arrived back in her hand.

'Thank you,' she murmured politely.

'My pleasure,' he answered, then shook her self-control by placing cool fingers beneath her chin and lifting it.

Their eyes clashed again—his filled with the glinting challenge of what was to come next. He was going to kiss her again, and she didn't think she could bear it.

Please don't, she wanted to say, but knew that she couldn't—because Parsons was standing there and Rafael would be angry if she rejected him in front of him. It was one of the rules by which they lived.

'You can treat me how you like when we are alone, but in front of others you maintain the status quo,' he'd said once, icy with anger because she'd flinched away from his touch at a dinner party. She remembered the punishing kiss which had followed so clearly that she had never dared to challenge that anger again—hence yet another reason why she rarely went anywhere with him.

She dragged in an unsteady breath. Her eyes dropped to his mouth, watching as it began to lower towards her own.

Parsons opened the front door and a blast of cold air hit them. She sucked in a shocked breath. Rafael tensed and tossed a slicing glance at the butler, then changed his expression with a rueful tilt to his upper lip.

Taking her arm, he walked her out of the house with a very dry, *'Grazie,'* to Nina's saviour.

Gino was standing by the rear door of the limousine. He waited until they were almost upon him before he swung it open so that Nina could sink inside.

The door closed, surrounding her in warmth and luxury leather. Rafael strode around the car to get in from the other side, and in seconds they were sweeping around the circular courtyard and onto the driveway, with Gino's familiar dark bulk dimmed by the screen of tinted glass that separated the front of the car from the rear.

A mingling of scents teased her nostrils—one light and subtle, the other spicy and dark. There were butterflies taking up residence low down in her stomach, and nervous tension sent the tip of her tongue on a slow tasting of her upper lip.

'Now we talk,' Rafael said, suddenly turning to look at her and catching her in the nervy little act. His eyes blackened. Her tongue-tip stilled. Tension cracked like a whip in the space between them and—

She felt his kiss again. Maybe Rafael did too. Because there was a single tight second when his own lips parted and she thought he was going to touch his lip with the tip of his tongue.

Erotic, it would have been—suggestive, inviting. They'd used to play games like that, so she knew exactly how it went.

Then an electronic beep hit the silence. Her tongue-tip disappeared and he was digging a hand into his jacket pocket. A second after that he was holding his cellphone to his ear.

'Ah, Fredo—*ciao*,' he greeted, and Nina's mouth changed shape into a very wry smile.

Rafael saw it and his eyes narrowed. His manner with Fredo altered to become short as he conducted a brief conversation in the Sicilian dialect that came naturally to both men.

'Why the wry smile?' he demanded, the moment the call had finished.

'Fredo must be counting himself fortunate to have caught you with your phone switched on for a change.' Maybe she did have a desire to use knives, Nina thought, as the slicing cut of her tone narrowed those dark eyes some more.

'Fredo knows I cannot always be at the end of a telephone,' he responded levelly. 'He's called you, looking for me?'

'Several times.' Nina nodded. 'It sounded—urgent.'

'He should control the urge to panic.'

'I would call it concern.'

'I would call it an imposition I don't much care for.'

She frowned, puzzled. 'I don't mind if he—'

'*I* mind, *cara*,' he inserted grimly. 'If Fredo needs a sympathetic shoulder to cry on let him use someone else's.'

'He did not cry on my shoulder,' she denied. 'He simply asked if I knew where you were because he needed to contact you and your phone was switched off. And how can you speak about him like that when he's supposed to be your closest friend?' she demanded. 'He's going through a really rough time at the moment. You should feel—'

'Sorry for him?' he put in. 'Trust me, it is dangerous to feel sorry for Fredo, and I advise you to heed that—for your own good.'

Suddenly it was Nina sensing knives being drawn. She stared at him as undercurrents of old issues began to ripple through the tension. He might be sitting there looking beautifully relaxed, but there was nothing relaxed about those hard features or the glint in those eyes he had fixed on her.

'This is a ridiculous conversation,' she said in the end, withdrawing from battle by sinking back into her seat.

'You think so?' he drawled. 'Fredo is a sucker for lost souls. That makes you and him a dangerous combination. Therefore he stays away from you or I will make sure that he does.'

'I suppose you're *not* a sucker for those same lost souls?' Nina countered, too stung by his implication that she was a lost soul not to retaliate. 'The Monteleone Trust was set up merely for its tax concessions, and the lost souls it gathers in don't really count?'

A frown lashed his brow. 'My name is listed on hundreds of charities.'

'But it heads only one. Why dismiss it as nothing special?'

He shifted tensely, turning his head away, but not before Nina had seen the vulnerable glint shoot across his eyes. He might hate to talk about it, but the Monteleone Trust was Rafael's big acknowledgement to his past.

It was a string of projects set up and designed to give troubled young men and women from a similar background to his own the opportunity to do something constructive with their lives. He employed only the very best to guide and encourage them, and Fredo was the best of the best. He too had known the same childhood as Rafael. His ideals were in complete sympathy with Rafael's ideals. And Rafael might prefer to sit here mocking Fredo's passion for *lost souls*, as he put it, but they were his lost souls too.

A sigh hissed from him. 'We were talking about you and Fredo.'

'You were. I was trying to change the subject.'

'You had lunch with him three days ago—'

Nina stared at him. 'Are you accusing me of something—again?' she dared to demand.

It was like teasing old issues to come out and show themselves. His lips thinned out, and his teeth, she suspected, were clenching behind them in an effort to keep those issues locked in. But they were there now, rattling away at her and reminding her why she hated him. And reminding him of things about her that he much preferred to forget.

'He is already halfway to falling in love with you. I would prefer it if he was not encouraged to make it more than that.'

She wanted to laugh because it was such a joke. 'We had lunch in Syracuse. We shared a bowl of pasta, not an interlude of untrammelled lust!'

The word *lust* turned those glinting eyes into lasers. If she could, this would be the point where Nina would get up and walk away from him.

'I don't know how you can sit there talking about Fredo like this when he has never been anything but loyal to you.'

'Men in love do strange things…'

'Is that so?' Her laugh escaped. It was short and derisive. 'That explains it, then.'

'Explains what?' he asked, and then, while she fought with the answer she knew was bubbling up inside her, 'Has he already made his feelings clear to you? Is that it?' he shot at her.

'You are such a hypocrite, Rafael,' she informed him coldly. 'I wonder sometimes how you manage to justify it to yourself.'

The car came to a stop then. Nina had never been more relieved about anything. Without waiting to listen to what else he had to say, she opened her door and stepped out into the crisp, cold night.

She was trembling all over, but she told herself they were shivers of cold and huddled into her coat.

Her grandfather's house was a tall, thin *palazzo* situated in one of the tiny squares in Syracuse. Lights blazed from the windows; cars lined the square. Nina had never felt less like going to a party, but the alternative was to finish what she had just started and she would not ruin her grandfather's birthday!

Rafael was striding around the car towards her. Gino had not even bothered to get out. The chauffeur could sense a heated row when it was taking place feet away from him, and was wisely keeping out of it.

Nina made for the house. As she reached the front door it swung open, flooding her with light, and she walked in with her head high and her legs trembling dangerously. A servant murmured polite greetings as he waited to take her coat. She could feel Rafael's anger as he waited for the servant to move away from her again.

Another door came open on the floor above, and the sounds of a party already in full flow poured out. As the servant moved away with her coat Nina turned towards the stairs which led up to the main salon, defiance running like fire in her veins—only to suddenly feel chilled to her very bones as one particular sound separated itself from all the rest.

Laughter.

It had always been able to do that, she was thinking dizzily. Had always managed to shine brighter than anyone else's laughter could.

Rafael arrived beside her, big and dark and angry because she'd spoken to him the way that she had. He caught hold of her arm again.

As he swung her to face him her eyes had already glazed, her skin prickling with rising nausea, her face turned so pale it took on a whole new dimension of paste.

He saw the change, and whatever angry retort was about to shoot from his lips altered. 'What's the matter?' he asked sharply.

'You bastard,' she whispered, and the fact that she was using that word to him of all people made it all the more potent.

CHAPTER FIVE

SHOCK rendered Rafael still for a second. Nina began to shake. It came again then, as clear as a lightly toned bell chiming out its presence—and Rafael heard it too.

A curse ripped from him. That curse said more to Nina than if he'd tossed out a full confession to her.

'You knew she was here and you didn't bother to tell me. How could you do this to me?' she breathed.

'She has as much right to be here as you do, Nina,' he returned grimly. 'A two-year exile from her home and family is long enough. Show a little compassion, for goodness' sake.'

Nina would have smiled at that if she was able—but she was incapable of doing anything right now.

Another sound from upstairs separated itself from the others. It was her grandfather's voice, calling her name. Looking up, Nina saw him standing looking down at her over the first floor balustrade. Rafael uttered another thick curse.

With her stomach churning out dire warnings and the rest of her clutched in bands of steel, Nina dredged up a smile from somewhere.

'Happy birthday, Nonno,' she called up to him, and began walking on legs that didn't feel real.

'Grazie piccola.' He beamed a smile back down to her. 'I do not feel like the seventy-year-old man people insist I am. But come up—come up,' he added impatiently. 'You are late. I was about to telephone your house to find out where you were. Good evening, Rafael, I am happy that you could make it…'

Rafael said nothing. He was tracking behind her up the long staircase and she could feel his anger and frustration hitting her rigid spine. Her grandfather didn't notice the missing answer; he didn't notice Nina's sickly pallor or her tension or tremors as he welcomed her into his arms.

He was too excited, his eyes flashing with it. 'Has Rafael told you about the surprise he delivered to me on his way home this afternoon?'

Rafael delivered—? Nina froze yet again.

'Have I put my big foot in it?' her grandfather responded sharply. 'Did he not tell you?'

Brazen it out, she told herself. Pretend you're ecstatic. 'Of course he told me,' Nina assured him—and smiled.

'Good—good.' Relief fluttered momentarily behind his excitement. Then he was fitting her slender frame beneath the crook of his arm. 'Then let us go in!'

The first person she saw when she stepped into the salon was her mother, her face looking whiter than the silk gown she wore. Louisa hurried forward, ostensibly to embrace her daughter, but the real reason was the hurried words she whispered. 'I knew nothing about this until I arrived here five minutes ago or I would have told you.'

'I know,' Nina said. It was all she could manage,

because her eyes had already found the real star of the show.

She was standing not far away, wearing purple for passion, beautiful, exotic, her dark hair floating around her exquisitely perfect but apprehensive face.

The first thing Nina felt was a rush of warm tenderness for this cousin who had once been her closest friend—until she reminded herself that the face which had spent the last two years fronting one of the biggest beauty campaigns did not do apprehensive. And the way Marisia lifted those anxious eyes up over Nina's shoulder to where Rafael stood, grim and silent, told her why she was playing the vulnerable one.

If he offered any reassurance then it did not alter Marisia's expression. She dropped those incredible dark eyes back to Nina's face. And what made the whole charade all the more sickening was that everyone present here believed that Nina had stolen Rafael from Marisia in the first place.

She was the original sinner in this room, and Marisia the one to be pitied.

Well, I can deal with that, Nina told herself. I prefer to be the sinner than the sinned upon.

And on that thought she drew on every bit of her strict English upbringing and put her mother to one side. 'Marisia,' she greeted her warmly. 'How very nice to see you here…' And she smiled.

How very nice indeed, Rafael thought grimly as he watched his wife run the gauntlet of everyone's curiosity to substantiate her greeting with the expected kisses on her cousin's cheeks.

Hypocrite.

That word was still sticking its sharp point into him. Nina had not used the word just for effect. Did she know? Could she know?

His attention switched to his mother-in-law, who was standing beside him wearing an expression that was more anxious than Marisia's as she watched the two cousins embrace. He hadn't thought much about Louisa's presence here; it would be expected that she attend her father's birthday party, but a week ago she had been in London, being wined and dined by a rich banker who'd been recently widowed.

Had Louisa seen—heard—something and passed that information on to Nina?

Sensing his eyes on her, Louisa glanced up, her dark eyes instantly growing cold. Her lips parted impulsively, then she had second thoughts about whatever it was she had been about to say and closed them again.

'Got something you want to tell me, Louisa?' he prompted smoothly.

'No,' was all that came out, and she returned her eyes to the embracing cousins.

'Good,' he said. 'For a moment there I really thought you were going to say something to me that you might regret later, when you'd had time to think about it.'

He was making subtle reference to the healthy amount of money he paid into her account each month, which kept Louisa's privileged lifestyle afloat.

She glanced back at him. 'You have eyes like a killer hawk,' she told him.

Rafael smiled, because he hadn't expected that comment. 'Windows to my soul, *cara*,' he confided.

Louisa shivered and looked away, again having received the message.

Her father turned towards them then—and beamed out a delighted grin. 'This must be the perfect birthday gift for an old man, to see those two together again like this,' he declared, as insensitive as ever to what was really going on around him. Then almost immediately he lost interest in his 'gift'. 'Rafael, if you have a few minutes I have a little something interesting I would like to—'

'Another time, Alessandro,' he cut in. 'I promised my wife I would not spoil your birthday, you see…'

With that said, Rafael left father and daughter standing there, knowing that Alessandro had received his message too. The old man now aware that Rafael knew what he was up to, and was not pleased about it. So he would keep out of his way for the rest of the evening.

Which was exactly what Rafael wanted him to do.

Nina's smile held without faltering throughout the next hour. She'd smiled when she greeted the beautiful Marisia like the prodigal come home again, and she shone over everyone else's curiosity and made them smile too. She talked and she laughed and she greeted each individual as if they all were warmly welcome prodigals. Uncles, aunts, her many other cousins—and friends of her grandfather who beamed beneath the warmth of her smile.

And she drank champagne by the gallon.

By the time they were called into dinner she was amazed she could still walk in a straight line.

Everyone took their places at the long table. Nina

found herself seated next to Rafael—with Marisia sitting directly opposite.

Oh, great, she thought—and smiled.

The first course arrived. Wine bottles chinked against slender-stemmed glasses. One of her male cousins was sitting on her other side, and she engrossed herself in conversation with him about—goodness knows what, until the poor guy was exhausted.

There was noise and fun and talking over talking— a meal enjoyed Sicilian-style.

Marisia wowed everyone with stories about her celebrity lifestyle, and Nonno inserted eager prompts that showed how closely he had been following Marisia's career.

Louisa was quiet.

So was Rafael.

'More wine please, darling,' Nina requested, holding out her empty glass to him for its third refill.

He had spent most of the awful dinner dividing his time between watching her from under brooding dark eyelashes and sending coded little messages across the table to Marisia. As his eyes fixed her with a steady look she knew he was going to refuse.

Try it, her own flashing blue invited him. Because I hate you and I am really warming up to causing a good scene by telling you how much I hate you—and she smiled.

His gaze flicked across the table to Marisia, and another one of those infuriating messages passed between the two of them.

Nina gave an impatient shake of her glass to regain his attention.

'Fill Nina's glass for her, someone,' her grandfather said.

Mouth pinned flat to his teeth, Rafael obliged, taking a wine bottle from its bed of ice and stretching out to pour some into her glass. The crisp dry white barely splashed the bottom. Nina stared ruefully into it—then at him. It was his turn to send a warning with his eyes telling her not to dare push it.

So she didn't. She turned her attention on Marisia instead. 'How long do you have with us before you need to go back to New York?'

It was intriguing to watch the little start she gave at being asked such an ordinary question. 'I will not be going back,' she said with a tense smile, and for the life of her could not hold Nina's deeply interested blue gaze.

Guilty conscience, Nina named it. And was impressed that Marisia had managed *not* to look at Rafael before she spoke.

'She is staying here with me over the Christmas period,' their grandfather put in. 'We mean to enjoy ourselves—heh, *cara*?'

'Yes.' Another tense smile was flicked his way. 'It feels so good to be home. I've missed you all so much…'

A flurry of 'we missed you too' rippled round the table. But for some reason the wave of assurance did not ease Marisia's unease. Her lovely olive-toned skin had gone pale, and her mouth was actually trembling. Nina even thought she could detect genuine apprehension in her cousin's dark eyes when she could not hold out any longer and threw yet another of those glances at Rafael.

Rafael in his turn did not move a muscle. When Nina allowed herself a quick glance at him she saw he was sitting there with his eyes carefully lowered, his glossy black eyelashes curling against his chiselled cheeks. It was as if he'd withdrawn his support, or whatever it was that Marisia looked for each time she looked at him.

Or maybe he was thinking of other things. Maybe he was hiding his eyes like that because he was seeing Marisia in his arms, in his bed.

Were they sleeping with each other?

Did she care?

Marisia uttered a strained little laugh. 'You might all change your minds about that in a minute,' she said tensely.

Silence followed—a hint of a warning that feathered itself down Nina's spine when she saw one of Rafael's hands curl into a fist. She looked back at her cousin and, like everyone else, waited for her to go on.

'I h-have something I need to tell you,' she continued unsteadily. 'I w-was going to leave it until after Christmas, but I don't think I can…' She paused yet again, to pull in a stifled breath. 'I've come home because I'm going to have a baby!' she finished with a defiant rush.

Shock threw itself around the table. Nina froze. Rafael straightened in his seat.

Alessandro Guardino was the first to recover, his eyes beetling a look down the table towards Marisia. 'And where is the father of this child while you sit here announcing this?' he demanded. 'Where is your wedding ring?'

'Th-there won't be a w-wedding,' Marisia informed him. 'H-he already has a wife, so I—'

Nina came to her feet with a jerk.

'Nina—' Louisa followed suit, her cry pained and anxious.

'Excuse me,' Nina whispered, and turned, almost staggering around her chair in her need to get away.

More chairs moved as others came to their feet. Pandemonium broke out. But she just kept on going, weaving an unsteady line towards the door and escape. Everything was moving in and out of focus. She had a horrible feeling she was going to faint.

'Stay where you are, Louisa,' Rafael's grim voice commanded.

'How could you be so cruel as to set her up for this?' she heard her mother whip back at him, and she almost sobbed in her need to get out before it all blew up.

She managed to get the door open, then headed like a dizzy drunk for the stairs. Her mind was sloshing about on a sea of champagne bubbles. It kept trying to toss up hard truths at her, but she blocked them out. She just needed to get out of there, she told herself frantically—away from those angry voices she could hear raising hell, away from those angry feet she could feel vibrating on the oak floor as they came after her.

She was halfway down the stairs when Rafael came to a stop at the head of them, and she knew why he'd pulled to a halt there. If he came after her she might stumble. It had happened to tragic effect once before. They'd rowed, she'd walked away, and he'd come after her to apologise.

The next thing she'd known she'd been falling— falling...

No. She pushed the rest of that memory away, along

with every other one trying to batter a hole in her head. Her feet made it to the ground floor and kept on going. She'd reached the front door before Rafael dared to let himself move at all.

Outside, the cold night air rushed into her lungs and she gulped at it. Instantly those champagne bubbles began fizzing and popping, flooding her bloodstream with pure alcohol, and she staggered.

A pair of hands grabbed her by the shoulders and grimly steadied her. 'I h-hate you,' she choked.

He said nothing. He just held her upright while she shivered and shook.

Gino had been parked across the square, but the moment he'd seen her step out of the house he had started up the engine and was already purring to a halt by her side. Rafael opened the rear door and bundled her into it, with no finesse, no striding round the car to get in from the other side. He simply followed her, forcing her to scramble out of his way.

Her coat landed on top of her. How he'd found time to get it, Nina had no idea, but she huddled into it as the car moved off.

Rafael sat beside her with a profile like granite.

'You knew that was coming, didn't you?' she bit out accusingly.

There was a pause, a rasp of a sigh, followed by a teeth-gritting 'Yes…'

CHAPTER SIX

NINA wondered if she was ever going to breathe again without hurting. 'So you set me up.'

Rafael turned his head. 'Your mother said something similar—as if it is a sin for someone else to have a baby while you are still grieving the loss of your own! Did it not occur to either of you that Marisia's present situation deserves your understanding and sympathy, not some dramatic exit staged to swing the sympathy all your way!'

He was angry on Marisia's behalf? Nina stared at him as if he had just crawled out from beneath a stone. 'You really are,' she breathed tautly, 'the most absolute bastard—to dare to expect understanding and sympathy from me when your mistress announces that she is having your baby!'

'Mistress?' The single word shot from his lips in stunned astonishment. 'I don't keep a mistress!'

'What do you call her then—your true love?'

He met that piece of flaying sarcasm with silence. Nina looked away, hating—*hating* him! How could he *do* this to her?

Her mouth began to tremble, her eyes to fill with hot tears. She clutched her coat to her with icy fingers and stared fixedly out of the car window, seeing through the layer of tears that they'd already left the lights of Syracuse behind them and were climbing the hill towards home.

Home. No place had ever felt less like home to her. She hated the house—hated the life she had been living there in a marriage that had never been anything but a huge pretence.

'I think you had better explain what the hell it is you are talking about,' he said finally.

'I know about you and Marisia,' she obliged, and wished that she'd said it the moment he'd stepped into her bedroom this afternoon. Then she would not have been exposed to the horror of tonight! Her head swung round, blue eyes stabbing into his taut profile. 'Did you think you could swan around London with her *without* someone I know seeing you together there?'

His first response was to turn his head to look at her, the next was to draw himself in. Danger suddenly lurked in those lean, hard features. The kind of danger that arrived when a man like him found himself backed into a tight corner he knew he was not going to get out of.

'Who was it?' he rapped out.

He wasn't even going to lie and deny it! Stomach-churning distress joined in with the rest of the mayhem taking place inside her.

'You know what, Rafael?' she said. 'It doesn't matter who told me, or even if I did know about the two of you before that staged scene you put me through tonight. The fact that she was there at all says that you must have given her your blessing, or my grandfather would not have dared let her in the house!'

It was all to do with priorities. Her grandfather might love Marisia, but he loved Rafael's money more.

A frown broke his rigid expression. 'What does that have to do with anything?'

'It has everything to do with me!' Nina cried. 'She is the woman you were in love with—the one you would have married if she had not walked out on you! To have given your consent for her to come back here means you have to have had contact with her. To have had contact with her means you broke a promise you made to me on our wedding day! To have broken that promise means that my feelings matter less to you than hers do—which you well and truly proved tonight.'

'You're crazy,' he breathed.

Maybe she was, Nina allowed. Maybe she had been out of her head for the last two years!

The car came to a stop. Reaching for the door, Nina pushed it open and scrambled out. As she ran up the shallow stairwell Parsons opened the front door.

'Good evening,' he greeted her. 'I did not expect you back so—'

'Close the door,' she instructed as she ran past him. 'I don't want him in here!'

With that she kept on going, dropping the coat in a black puddle on the floor at the foot of the stairs. She was trembling and shaking and the champagne was still fizzing.

The door did close, but it wasn't Parsons who did it. 'Nina!' Rafael roared after her. 'Go up those stairs the way you came down your grandfather's and I will kill you—if you don't do it to yourself first!'

She stopped two steps up and twisted to glare at him

across the length of chequered flooring. He was standing there in his black dinner suit and bow tie looking as handsome as hell, yet so pale she knew what he was envisaging.

Maybe it was the look on his face that made her bend to take her shoes off. Then again maybe it wasn't, because the next thing she did was launch the damn shoes towards his still frame.

'Just get out of my house!' she yelled at the top of her trembling voice as the black patent leather shoes landed just short of their target.

Then she turned and ran up the curving staircase in a heaving, stumbling mess of anger and tears.

Rafael tried telling himself he should be pleased to see that she'd turned on all her emotions again. But pleasure was not the emotion he was feeling as he watched her fly up that damn staircase while her coat lay at the bottom like a grim reminder of how she had looked that day she had landed in a final heartbreaking twist of slender limbs.

He hated this house. He hated that damn staircase!

As soon as she had safely reached the top, one gut-wrenching set of feelings were swapped for a different set, and it broke him free of his grim stasis.

Marisia—his mistress?

The child she was carrying was—his?

He began striding after her, stepping over the shoes and the discarded coat, leaving the butler standing by the door trying his best to appear as if he had not witnessed that little scene.

But Parsons *had* witnessed it, which only infuriated

Rafael all the more. He took the stairs two at a time, arriving on the upper landing as her bedroom door slammed. With dire intent burning like a blister on his pride, he strode through the archway, feeling as if his face had been carved from stone it was so rigid with anger.

His fingers grasped the handle; he threw open the door and stepped inside. She was standing in the middle of the room with her arms wrapped tightly around her. He slammed the door.

'Right, let us get a few facts straight,' he gritted. 'Marisia is *not* my mistress. She is *not* having my child!'

Nina responded by turning for the bathroom. Bright balls of pain and anger were propelling themselves to the backs of her eyes.

She took just one step before a pair of strong arms came around her and scooped her off her feet.

Her shrill cry of protest earned her nothing. 'Oh, no, you don't,' he gritted. 'Not this time.'

With a lithe twist of his body followed by two strides he tossed her onto the bed, then followed her down there, a solid package of lean, hard, long-limbed masculinity pinning her to the bed.

She gasped at the shock of it, and found herself staring into black holes for eyes and a tensely parted mouth that was so close she could actually taste it. Awareness rushed through her like a raging torrent, every sense she possessed leaping to life at the return of a physical contact they had been denied for months. She tingled and pulsed—and despised herself for letting it happen.

'Get off me, you brute,' she choked out thickly.

'I will when you promise to stay still and listen,' he said huskily, but she knew he wasn't going anywhere.

Like her, he was aware that this was the closest they'd been in months—and she could see by the look in his eyes that he liked it. She could feel every tensing, flexing, sensational muscle he possessed, and the worst part about it was that he could feel every one of hers.

His jacket lay spread open on either side of her; his long fingers were buried in her hair as they cupped her head. Her skirt had rucked up around her hips and the heels of her hands were braced against his shirt-front, to stop him coming any closer, her tense fingers fighting to relax into contact with the familiar warm firmness they knew waited a tantalisingly small inch away.

She sucked in some air and her breasts made that contact. A panic of pleasuring frissons set her fighting him for all she was worth.

She pushed at his chest and bucked her hips in an effort to dislodge him. She gasped and choked and spat out words she had never used in her life. When nothing made him move she hit out at him with her fists, then tried using her nails—until he denied them the chance to do any damage by capturing both wrists and pinning them to the bed above her head.

Her eyes flashed blue lightning at him and her lips quivered. 'You are a faithless, cheating liar and I hate you,' she hissed.

'The only liar I know is the one who told you I'm sleeping with your cousin!'

'So you took her to our apartment for a chat, did you?' she flashed up at him. 'After you seduced her across a candlelit dinner table for two!'

The sarcasm clicked. He went still, his eyes hooded over.

Nina began to struggle free with new impetus.

'Stop it while I think.' His strength subdued her.

'You're crushing me.'

'No, I'm not,' he denied, making her aware of the way he was evenly distributing his weight between two key points, his bent arms and his legs placed on either side of her own.

'Louisa,' he murmured in the end. 'She saw us together and rushed straight back here to tell you what she'd seen. What a pleasure it must be to have such a caring mother,' he mocked cynically. 'I think I would rather have an indifferent one, like my own.'

At last he moved away, rolling onto his back beside her to stare grimly at absolutely nothing.

Nina sat up then, and surprised herself by doing nothing either. 'She's her father's daughter,' she said.

'Ah, si,' he drawled, as if that explained everything.

Which it did. Louisa had not come chasing up here to surprise her daughter with the pleasure of her company for lunch. She hadn't even come bearing grim warnings about what Rafael was doing in London for Nina's benefit. She'd done it because she'd seen her allowance at risk and had wanted to jolt Nina out of her apathy and get her to fight for her ailing marriage before they all lost their only income source.

'What it is to be a billionaire,' Rafael murmured bitterly, making Nina aware that he was thinking more or less the same thing. 'It makes you so popular your head could swell if you so allowed it.'

'You're as guilty as everyone else of using your money to get what you want,' she threw back.

His hand came out, long fingers trailing lightly down

her arm. 'I had to buy you, *cara*,' he murmured huskily. 'It was the only way you would have me.'

Nina pulled her arm away, then rubbed where his fingers had been. 'Stop trying to divert the subject.'

'This is the subject,' he argued. 'I never wanted Marisia. I *always* wanted you.'

'Gosh, it showed,' she responded bitterly. 'Especially when you told me you did not want children—having told her that you did.'

She got up then, feeling sick again, restless and—hurt.

'I never said that.' He sat up. 'Why would I say that to Marisia when I knew it wasn't possible?'

He had a—point to which Nina had no answer. 'Well, you didn't bother to tell *me* that you thought you couldn't have children. Maybe you told her that you could because you thought it was what she wanted to hear.'

'If I did then I made a lousy error of judgement,' he denounced, 'because Marisia does not want children. She cannot bear the thought of them. She does not even want the child she carries!'

Nina swung round. 'What do you mean?' she demanded.

'Exactly what I say.' He got to his feet, angry fingers dragging the bow tie loose. 'Marisia does not want the baby.' His shirt button was loosened next. 'I spent the last few days talking her out of aborting it. She agreed in the end—hence tonight's announcement.' The jacket came next and was dropped onto the bed.

Nina stared at him, looking at what he had just said from a completely different perspective. 'And how long have you been in such close contact with her that she felt she could confide all of this in you?'

'Ah,' he sighed. 'I think am digging myself a hole here.'

'You're so right you are,' Nina agreed.

He strode across the room towards the drinks tray. 'I have never been out of contact with her—OK?'

The defensive *OK* ripped her heart in two. Did he love Marisia so much that he had not been able to keep away from her?

'She was struggling in New York. Homesick—miserable,' he pushed on as he uncapped a decanter. 'She got into an affair with this wealthy businessman, then found out too late that he had a wife and children tucked out of way somewhere. She decided that London was the best place to have an abortion. We—bumped into each other. She told me what she was about to do.'

'Bumped into each other?' Nina repeated. 'As in—by accident?'

He grimaced. 'She called me,' he added with a shrug. 'Said she was in trouble and needed help.' Cognac splashed into a glass. 'We arranged to meet for dinner and she told me about the baby then. You know my past,' he added grimly. 'What right has any woman to deny a child its right to survive?'

'What right does any man have to deny his own child?'

'Marisia's baby is not mine,' he repeated angrily.

'I was talking about my—*our* baby!' Nina shrilled. 'You denied responsibility for that!'

'And you know why!' he thrust back at her.

'Because you had a vasectomy ten years ago, therefore I had to be the faithless one who'd taken a lover?' she lashed back. 'I know what you prefer to believe, Rafael.'

'I was still prepared to love it as my own.'

'And hate me all you could.'

'Daniel Fraser was in your life before I came into it. He had an emotional grip on you that I could not break.'

'Oh, you broke it,' she assured him. 'You bought out his company and had me dismissed!'

'After he seduced you into bed to get his revenge on you for marrying me!'

'Revenge?' she repeated. 'Well, thanks for letting me know that I'm only good for a quick lay in the name of revenge!'

'I did not mean it like that.' He sighed.

'You married me to get your revenge on Marisia. Daniel seduced me in revenge for marrying you!' She laughed because it was so ridiculous to hear it said. 'I suppose I am seducing Fredo to get revenge on you for turning me into a cheap little tramp!'

He put the glass to his lips again and drank, his taut profile ripping her to shreds because she could see from it that was exactly what he did think!

'Very Sicilian,' she derided shakily. Then, because she just could not stand here listening to this any longer, 'Get out of here, Rafael,' she said, 'before I really say something you won't like to listen to.'

'Say it,' he invited. 'At least we are talking, which is infinitely better than the silence we've enjoyed for the last six months!'

Without warning the lid came flying off her temper. Before she knew what she was going to do she'd closed the gap between them and had snatched the glass from his hand. It landed with a crash back on the tray.

'OK, you asked for it.' She looked up at him, blue eyes full of burning contempt. 'Revenge is a fine word to fall from the lips of the man who took revenge on his own body by denying it the right to reproduce!'

He went pale as the hard accusation hit home. 'Only a fool would want to pass on my genetic fingerprint.' He turned his back to her.

'You don't *know* your genetic fingerprint!' Nina lashed at that rigidly set back. 'You only fear what it might be!'

'Is this leading somewhere?' he bit out tautly.

'Yes!' she cried. 'Because you fear it so much that you could not even bring yourself to look it in the face when I got pregnant! If you had then you would have started to ask questions about yourself! It's common knowledge that a vasectomy can reverse itself—that's the power of our instinct to reproduce! But did you check that out? No.' she said, and began to shiver. 'You preferred to believe I could sleep around like a whore.'

'I did check it out...'

'What?' he'd spoken so low in his chest that she thought she'd misheard him. Then he flexed his shoulders and she knew she had not misheard a thing. 'When?' she said, and because she needed to look at him when he answered she stepped round in front of him. What she saw written on his face dragged the breath from her throat. 'You know, don't you?' she heaved out breathlessly. 'You *know* the baby I lost was your baby!' She began to tremble all over her. 'Do you feel bad about that, Rafael, or are you all the more relieved that it's gone?'

'Don't say that!' he rasped. 'I never wished it any harm!'

She hit him so hard it rocked him on his feet.

CHAPTER SEVEN

TEARS flashed like blue lightning across her eyes as she watched her fingerprints stand out on his cheek. She did not regret hitting him, but she did not want to look at that arrogant face wearing her mark of contempt so she turned away.

'Get out of my house,' she said thickly. 'I never want to see you again so long as I live.'

It took every bit of withered strength she had left in her shaking limbs to turn and walk away from him.

'No.' He sounded gruff and harsh. She was not surprised to find herself caught by the shoulders again. 'I want you to listen,' he rasped, then let free with a string of thick, tight curses when his touch turned her to stone.

It was his turn to step around her so he could look her full in her icy white face. 'I am not going to let you shut me out now you have managed to remember that I do exist—faults and all,' he warned.

It was the *faults and all* part that made her unbend a little. The knowledge that he knew he had some deep personal issues that made him impossible to live with.

'All right, say what you want to say,' she invited

stiffly, folding her arms beneath her breasts and locking her eyes on the floor.

His second string of soft curses turned all women from victims into ruthless tormentors. 'How you can think that a man like me would want to involve myself with two women at the same time is beyond me— No, don't cry, *cara*,' he said gruffly. 'If you let those tears fall then I will not be responsible for what I—'

'Just talk!' she cut in thickly.

He sucked in some air, his fingers tightening their grip on her arms. 'I took the test twice,' he said. 'The first time the result was inconclusive, and because it came only a couple of weeks after you told me you were pregnant I was happy to hang on to my version of the truth. I was scared that I might have made the biggest mistake in my life, so it suited me to push all the blame onto you.'

'My hero,' she mocked him.

He let go of her, swung away tensely, then immediately swung back again. 'Do you want the truth or some dressed-up version that makes me appear bigger than I am?' he lashed at her. 'You went away with Daniel Fraser for the weekend!'

'It was a business convention he was my boss and the whole firm was there!'

'The whole firm did not stop him from getting into your room!'

'He came to collect my suitcase!'

'I came to collect you!' he thrust back at her. 'And found myself having to break up a bloody clinch! He said, 'Nice having you, Nina,' before my fist was in his face!'

'I told you—he tried it on but that was all. Nothing else happened!'

'And I did not believe it!'

'Did not *want* to believe it.'

'Did I suggest the dressed-up version would sound better for me? My apologies.' He bowed stiffly. 'I was wrong. I still come out of it looking like the fool. And watch those tears,' he tagged on when he saw them fill her eyes again. 'Because I'm still hovering on the brink of saying to hell with this and throwing you back on the bed!'

Nina heaved in a deep breath, feeling her breasts quiver against her crossed arms—as if they preferred the bed option too!

'So you took the test and it was inconclusive?' she prompted, in an effort to get this back on track.

He nodded, then pushed his hands into his trouser pockets and drew himself in. 'We left London and came here to live. You walked around this house like a wounded animal and I hated it,' he went on thickly. 'We did not look at each other; we did not even speak!'

For weeks it had gone on, Nina recalled bleakly. Weeks and weeks of feeling like a stranger to herself. He'd told her he'd had a vasectomy. And then he'd told her why. 'I don't want children. I never want children!'

'Well, tough luck, Rafael,' she'd said. 'Because I am having your baby, whatever you think or want or believe…'

'In the end I could stand it no longer,' he continued. 'I took a hard look at what we were doing to each other and decided that if I wanted our marriage to survive I was going to have to swallow my pride and tell you I could forgive and forget, that I wanted to put the past aside and try again…'

And he'd told her with enough stiff-necked coldness to put an icy chill on her flesh, Nina recalled.

'You flew at me in a rage, then rushed out of this room vowing you were going to leave me. I went after you, knowing I had made a mess of it. You were already on the stairs. I said something—I don't know what…'

'I'm sorry,' he'd said. *'I did not mean that the way it came out…'*

'You turned to respond, but the front door flew open and your grandfather walked in,' he went on. 'As you spun back to look at him you stumbled off the top step—'

Nina put a hand up to cover her eyes. 'Please—don't say any more,' she begged.

'But I have to say it,' he insisted. 'It was my fault! I moved too late to stop you from falling. You lost the baby. Now I watch you take that fall every night in my sleep!'

'And you think that I don't?' Her hand dropped away again. He was standing in front of her, big and tense, with the agony of guilt carving grooves in his face. 'Do you think you are the only one to carry blame around?' she questioned. 'I was the careless one! I was the one who didn't watch my step! I was the stupid one who let you get to me the way that you did!'

'That is the whole point.' He reached for her again, long fingers curling over her slender arms. 'You might pretend to be the cool English rose, but you have so much Sicilian passion running riot inside you that you are a danger to yourself! I knew that. I should have backed off when you started shouting, then the fall would not have happened.'

'Well, don't worry about it. You backed off afterwards,' she said bitterly. 'So far back that you hardly came home—and you took a lover to keep you company at the same time!'

Dio,' he rasped. 'I did not take a lover—have you heard anything I've said? I stayed away because you coped better when I was not here to remind you. I— Oh, don't, dammit,' he groaned, when he saw the tears arriving yet again.

Then it came—the muttered, 'What the hell?' And the next thing she knew she was lifted up hard against him, with his arms wrapped around her and his mouth taking driving possession of the first sob as it broke on her lips.

It was a hellish kind of heaven. She hated him so much, yet her arms hooked around his neck and clung so tightly there was no way he could break free. She sobbed and she whimpered and she kissed him back with a passion that sang like a shrill tune in her head. When he managed to drag his mouth away she buried her face in his shoulder and sobbed like a baby.

He didn't like it. She could tell that by the way he stood so tense and silent while she sobbed.

'You know what you need?' he rasped out then.

Nina kept her face buried in his shoulder and shook her head.

'You need me,' he told her. 'All of me. Wrapped around you, inside you, naked flesh, naked passion— how else are you going to get rid of all this grief?'

'I want to hate you,' she mumbled on another sob.

'And you hate to want me. I know,' he grated, then he turned and did what he'd been threatening to do—returned them both to the bed. He covered her mouth again, taking her sobs as his own while she clung and let him.

She let him stroke her body and remove her dress. She let him kiss her where he wanted, let him suck gently on her breasts through the sheer black teddy and let him slide long fingers between her legs. And he did it all so carefully and sombrely that the tears began running down her cheeks again.

'Do you want me to stop?' His voice, like the finger he trailed across her wet cheek, was gentle and grim.

She shook her head, her hand still clutching his nape because the rest of her was beginning to float. 'Take me away with you,' she whispered.

There wasn't a moment when he questioned where she wanted to be taken to. The breath feathered from him as with a solemn gentleness he drew the teddy from her body and whispered it down her legs. Her knees came up, her toes curling inside her silk stockings as she curved herself into him. Her mouth hunted his, lips soft and trembling and desperately needy, touching and tasting while he dealt with the stockings too.

It felt good to be naked. It felt good to feel his hand moulding her breasts. When he moved away so he could take off his own clothes she watched him through big blue sombre eyes that kept his own eyes sombre and his movements tense.

No man had a body like Rafael. The broad shoulders, the wide chest, the light covering of hair that arrowed down his long golden torso to the flat plain between his narrow hips. When aroused, as he was now, he was magnificent, and when he eased himself on top of her it was the most wonderful feeling on earth. All hard muscle and living warmth, and a breathtakingly seductive and overpowering strength.

She looked into his face and saw the man of her dreams there. Loving or hating him, that dream never changed. I still love you, she thought, and hoped she did not say the words out loud.

He kissed her so gently that she thought maybe she had. He kissed and touched and stroked her where she needed him to, and eventually encouraged her to do the same to him. It was so long since she'd tracked her fingers over his flesh and watched him shudder in response, watched his eyes close with pleasure when her fingers closed around his sex….

The tears had long gone—driven away by the first probe of a sensual finger that arched her spine and then allowed it to relax again. He captured one of her breasts, rolling the tight rosebud nipple around his tongue then sucking gently until she groaned out a breathless protest, then he moved to the other breast.

Then it all suddenly changed. And it happened so fast that she didn't see it coming. His mouth came up to fuse with hers in a fierce, deep hunger, and at the same moment he located her G spot and turned the rolling waves of gentle passion into a driving, racing, turbulent storm.

She groaned and gasped and arched and panted. She scored her nails down his back and he took her, ruthlessly and without mercy, to the peak—only to stop and let her drop down again. When she opened her eyes to accuse him of teasing she met with raw desire, lashing his skin to his facial bones, and she knew what was coming just before he made that first deep silken thrust.

It was the difference between slow, sensual foreplay and hot, physical sex. He could indulge her for hours, but when he flipped over the edge he went without warning.

He needed it now, needed it all, and he needed it voraciously.

Each powerful thrust was deeper than the preceding one, and her muscles grabbed and held on, then quivered each time he withdrew to begin the next stroke. When she cried out with pleasure he shuddered; when she quivered he shuddered. When she shouted at the top of her voice, *'Please—!'* he strapped her to him with his arms and increased the pace. And he kept on increasing until he felt the familiar sensation building through her. Quickly the feeling overtook the thrusts, and she became lost in that electric world of pure sensation.

Coming down afterwards was like trying to swim against the flow of a river. Her heart wouldn't stop racing, and her blood was rushing so fast through her veins that she thought she could hear it. She tingled and shook and felt him still pulsating inside her. Her dry mouth and throat ached, because she still could not control her breathing.

'And that,' Rafael murmured huskily, 'is having all of me—wrapped around you and inside you.'

While they still lay in a tangle of trembling limbs, recovering from their most intense experience yet, Nina could not argue with his husky-voiced comment.

His warm mouth moved against her shoulder. She shrugged it away. 'Tell me about the second test you had,' she prompted.

He went still, then uttered a sigh and carefully withdrew so he could ease himself away. Then he rolled onto his back beside her on the bed.

'Last week,' he said abruptly. 'When the desire to exonerate you of everything grew strong enough to make me want an excuse to crawl to you on my knees and beg your forgiveness.'

'It took you six months to get there?'

His eyes flashed darkly. 'Do you want to hear this or not?'

'Yes,' she said.

He took a deep breath. 'As soon as I found out the result I was coming straight back here to tell you—then Marisia called with her news and told me what she intended to do.'

'I still can't stand to think of you seeing her behind my back.'

'Ditto you and Fredo,' he countered grimly. 'He is fresh out of a serious relationship. The last thing he needs is to see a door open to your broken heart, giving him ideas about two broken hearts making a whole one.'

'It isn't like that,' she protested. 'He's nice—he's your friend. We had lunch a couple of times and we talked about anything but broken hearts!'

'He told me to my face that I do not deserve you,' Rafael told her. 'He said that if I had any feelings for you at all I would let you go, so someone else could give you what I obviously could not. Who do you suppose he was thinking about when he offered that advice?'

'When did he say that?' she gasped, lifting her head to stare at him.

His face was like rock again. 'A couple of weeks ago,' he added with a shrug.

Curiosity had Nina levering herself up a bit further so she could capture his guarded eyes. 'He worried you,' she murmured silkily. His mouth flattened into a straight line. 'He planted the idea that I might actually give up on you altogether. You didn't like it, so you forced yourself to retake the test!'

'It was time.'

'You were scared and jealous!'

'I thought we were talking about Marisia!' he rasped.

'Oh, yes,' Nina murmured, and subsided again.

He heaved in yet another deep breath. 'She was frightened of what the family would think of her and saw abortion as her only way out,' he continued. 'You know what it's like here, Nina. There is still a heavy stigma attached to unmarried mothers. I delayed my trip by a few days so I could try and talk her out of it. It was not easy, and I did not dare leave her behind in London while I came here to you because I could not be sure she wouldn't change her mind. So I brought her with me—made her promise she would think about it over Christmas before she decided what she was going to do. She wasn't supposed to blurt it out tonight.'

'Then why did she?'

'Because she's a crazy woman—I don't know!' He sighed. 'I did not hang around long enough to find out!'

'Or because she wanted you tied down while she had the rest of us there as witnesses. If I knew about your affair with her then how many other people at that table knew?'

'This is going in circles.'

'Because I am still not convinced that her child is not your child?' She sat up. 'One mistake can easily become two mistakes, *caro*,' she said deridingly. 'Especially if you took so long to have your precious test! That makes the rest of this just—wallpaper!'

'If you want proof, *cara*—' he threw the same tone back at her. '—then you are going to have wait seven months. But I *will* prove it! I do not sleep around!'

'Neither do I!'

'All right—' He held up his hands. 'So I deserve all of this.'

The sound of a car coming up the drive caught their attention. Nina snaked off the bed and went to the window, tugging back the edge of the curtain, then releasing a sigh.

'I think you are going to have to prove it sooner than you thought,' she murmured, and turned to look at him. 'My grandfather is here,' she explained.

CHAPTER EIGHT

IT WAS like watching a light switch off, then come back on again to reveal a completely different man. 'She set me up.'

Realization was finally beginning to hit him.

'She's very good at it.'

'Her motive?' He climbed off the bed.

Nina could only offer an empty shrug. 'Regret for walking out on you? Or that good old motive revenge—on me this time, for jumping into her place?'

'She did not walk out on me.' Rafael frowned as he reached for his trousers. 'We did not have the kind of relationship either could walk away from. But I did tell her I was in love with you.'

'Me—?' Nina stared at him. 'Why would you tell her a lie like that?'

'It was not a lie.' Her huff of scorn made him grimace as he closed his trouser zip.

'I don't recall the word *love* coming into anything you said when you suggested we marry.'

'It would have seemed less of a blow to my pride if you'd turned down a simple business deal than if you'd turned me down. You're so...' A hand came out, long fingers making a helpless gesture. 'Special,' he finished huskily.

It was like being hit by one too many revelations. Nina sank down on to her dressing stool and then just stared. Did she believe him?

He was standing there looking like a man who'd recently enjoyed a woman inside and out. His hair was ruffled, his mouth was wearing that sexy glow of too many hot kisses—but did that collate with a man in love?

'I think you're pulling rabbits out of a hat now,' she said.

'Meaning what?' He sent her a curious look.

She shifted restlessly, because she wasn't exactly sure what she meant—only that... 'I have this horrible feeling that I am being manipulated,' she said in the end.

Car doors slammed then—several of them—bringing Nina back to her feet.

'No,' Rafael said gruffly. 'You stay here.'

'But he's—'

'Sicilian. I know,' he nodded grimly. 'Well, so am I—I think,' he added with a wry smile.

It was the first time she had ever heard him actually mock himself like that. It brought tears to her eyes, which was silly—but it did.

'What if he—?'

Grabbing up his shirt, he walked over to her and settled it across her shoulders. 'Just think about this while I'm down there,' he suggested huskily. 'We all use manipulation in one form or another. At the moment I am fighting for my marriage, and I am prepared to do anything to save it. But lying to you is not one of those things. There has already been enough of that. So I am telling you, *cara*, I have been in love with you since I first set eyes on you, and if you can bring yourself to believe that then we can deal with whatever else comes at us.'

'That is supposing I love you back.'

His eyes took on a glow. 'You are a tough lady when you want to be.' He sighed. Then he grinned and kissed her—once—briefly and was gone, leaving her with the itchy feeling that he *knew* she loved him— had always known…

The sound of knocking on the front door echoed through the hallway. Rafael was striding down the stairs just as Parsons was opening the door. The butler was barely given time to step to the side before Alessandro Guardino and his two sons were shouldering their way inside.

'Good evening again, Alessandro,' Rafael greeted him. 'What brings you away from your own birthday celebrations?'

All three Guardino men came to a stop when they saw him. Bare-chested and shoeless, and with his trousers resting low on his waist, he should have cast a vulnerable figure—but he didn't. Whoever his parents had been, they had endowed him with the kind of physique that intimidated other men.

It took the old man several seconds to deal with that before he took a threatening step forward. 'I want a word with you,' he gritted. 'You have been playing my granddaughters for fools.'

Parsons was about to do his usual and melt away, but Rafael stopped him with the lift of a hand. 'Wait,' he said quietly. 'Our—guests will not be staying long.'

Without a word the butler stayed perfectly still by the

open door. The three Guardino men moved forward, their expressions pouring scorn on Rafael's idea of back-up in a fist fight.

'If you think *he* is going to stop us from killing you, then you are a fool,' Alessandro jeered.

'You have a point,' Rafael conceded. 'But I think Gino could sway the odds my way.' And he lifted his eyes as his bodyguard stepped in through the front door. Built as wide as he was tall, Gino walked across the hall and went to stand beside Rafael.

All three Guardino men went very still.

'Now,' Rafael said, 'I think you had better explain why you feel the need to kill me.'

'You know why, you bastard.'

Strange, Rafael thought, but being called a bastard by this man was nothing like being called one by his wife. It must be the English accent that made the difference. Nina made the word sound so—sexy.

He smiled.

'This is not a joke!' Alessandro shouted.

'Too damn right, it isn't,' Rafael agreed, his face suddenly hardening. 'You had better explain what it is I am being accused of before I get Gino to throw you all out.'

Alessandro's sons were eyeing up the bodyguard and wondering if the two of them could take him. Don't try it, Rafael silently advised them. Gino had been known to wrestle five angry men to the ground.

'You are the one who made Marisia pregnant!'

'And you believe that?'

'She has brought shame on the family—you are her cousin's bastard husband!'

There was that word again. Rafael did not like it. He frowned. Beside him Gino flexed his muscles. He did not like the word either, since he wore the same label himself.

'Your penchant for backing the wrong horse is showing again, Alessandro, so take care what you say to me or you may alienate the source which usually bails you out!'

The old man stiffened at the reminder—and the threat. But this was a matter of honour, and in any Sicilian household family honour had to come before everything else.

'My own daughter confirms that she has seen you together! How do you explain that?'

'Louisa, like the rest of you, should learn to think before leaping to conclusions. I have no desire to touch Marisia. She turned me cold two years ago and she turns me cold now.'

'That's a lie. You were going to marry her.'

'You offered her, Alessandro, as a bargaining chip in lieu of the money you owed me. I politely declined.'

The old man went red. 'Only because you saw Nina and decided you wanted her instead.'

'Well, I can't argue with that.'

'Nina knows that you are the father of Marisia's child! It is the reason the poor girl ran from my house!'

Rafael said nothing. The truth was the truth after all.

The old man read that silence as a crack in his argument. 'She must be deeply hurt.'

'It is understandable.'

'You have been playing her for a fool—you have dishonoured her and the Guardino family. We have come to take her home with us.'

'Nina is already home,' Rafael pointed out.

'We demand to see her!' Angry frustration was beginning to set in. 'For all we know you might have hurt her again, like you did the last time when you threw her down the stairs!'

Danger raised its head suddenly, and everyone sensed it, even Rafael himself. 'I am going to give you a very good piece of advice now, Allesandro, and I suggest that you heed it.' He began walking forward, his steps slow and measured across the chequered floor. 'Leave this house now, while I still have some respect for you. You are, after all, my wife's grandfather, and you do care for her—which is the part I still respect. But if you say one more word I will probably hit you, and then we will both lose respect—for ourselves.'

As he moved closer all three men started backing, and the fact that they were doing it while Gino remained where he was, made a point that hammered itself home. There wasn't one of them witnessing this who didn't see that Rafael in this mood was strong enough for all three Guardino men.

'I'm an old man,' Alessandro blustered. 'My granddaughter would never forgive you if you laid a hand on me.'

'Precisely,' Rafael agreed. 'Which is why I am asking you to leave.'

'She deserves better than you.'

Another point Rafael had no argument with.

'Don't kid yourself that this is the end of it.' The door opening was now between them and him. 'We will be back tomorrow—with more of us.'

'I will look forward to it,' Rafael said. Then quietly and calmly closed the door.

When he turned round to face his two companions he discovered both had not moved at all. It was interesting, he mused, how danger emanated from within. He could feel it himself as he stood here. Was he pale? He felt pale, as if danger had leeched all the warmth from his blood.

He looked at the stairs. The stairs Nina had fallen down. He saw it happen again—watched her slip on her spindly heels then stumble, listened to her cries and his own as she rolled.

He flicked a glance at Gino. 'Make sure they leave,' he said.

With a nod the bodyguard eased out of the stasis holding him and disappeared towards the back of the house, meaning to carry out the task by stealth.

Parsons still had not moved a muscle, yet in some odd way Rafael knew he was not standing there like that because he was afraid to move. Too undignified, he thought, and would have smiled if he were able.

When he began walking towards the stairs again Parsons spoke. 'I will lock up now, sir, if you don't mind,' he said.

Rafael nodded, then paused with one foot on the first stair. 'Do you like living in this house, Parsons?' he asked curiously.

For the first time since he'd known him Rafael saw the butler's eyes give an anxious flash, as if sensing a trap. 'I am content to live where Mrs Monteleone lives, sir,' the butler replied.

Which did not answer the question. 'But would you care if we all left here and never came back?'

The *we all* eased some tension out of Parsons's shoulders. 'No, sir,' he said.

Rafael nodded, looked around him for a few seconds, then came to a decision. 'How long will it take you to make the house safe to leave?'

'No time at all, sir. Will an hour be too soon?'

'An hour sounds about perfect,' Rafael approved.

The butler was turning away, but he paused. 'If you don't mind me saying so, sir, it will do Mrs Monteleone good to get away from here.'

All I have to do is convince *her* of that, Rafael thought, and he continued up the stairs feeling every nerve-end he possessed cringe, as they always did when he walked these stairs.

When he stepped into her room she was standing by the window, watching the red taillights of her grandfather's car make their way down the hill towards Syracuse.

But she was still wearing his shirt.

'They will come back,' she said, without turning.

'I know.' Crossing the room to stand behind her, he slid his hands around her waist and gently drew her back against him. 'How much did you overhear?' he asked.

'Most of it,' she said. 'I don't want you to hurt them,' she added, and he smiled, because it was good to know that she realised he could do so if he wanted to.

'I like your grandfather,' he admitted. 'He might be a reckless rogue with my money, and he uses his connections with me to his own advantage, but he loves his family. When the chips were down he came here willing to sacrifice my money for your honour.'

'He believes what Marisia has said.'

'The point is, Nina—do you believe her?'

Her reply was to turn and snake her arms around his neck. 'I just want all of this to go away—now.'

It was not the answer he had wanted, and it showed in the way he frowned. 'I'm going to give you two choices,' he said. 'You can get dressed and I will have Gino drive you back to your grandfather's house. Or you can get dressed and come with me, and we will retreat to a safer place until the fuss has—'

'I go where you go!' Her arms tightened their hold on him.

She sounded like the butler, he thought. But that was all it was—a brief thought—because his attention was shifting to other, more seductive things. She had the warm, supple feel of a recently loved woman, and the bloom of that loving still lay soft on her lips and in the darkened blue of her eyes.

His senses stirred, and Nina saw it happen. The frown softened out of his hard features and his eyes took on that dark, sensual look as he studied her mouth. Her lips parted and her fingernails curled into his nape. She moved that bit closer, drawn by the heat of his body and the promise of what it could make her feel.

'We leave for London in an hour,' he murmured.

'OK,' she agreed.

His fingers moved on her waist, crushing fine cotton as he pressed her close. 'That means we don't have time for this.'

'OK,' she said again, not really believing him. He would *make* time. That was what Rafael did; he turned the world on its head to suit his requirements. 'I'll go and get dressed, then…'

Like hell you will, those black eyes said, and his mouth took her mouth by storm.

CHAPTER NINE

TWO hours later they were boarding a helicopter. It was midnight, and the clear night sky was alive with stars. As the helicopter lifted into the air Nina glanced back at the house, all shrouded in darkness now.

'Will you miss it?' Rafael asked quietly.

'The house? No,' she replied without hesitation, and turned away from it.

An hour after that they were seated on a chartered private jet.

Nina slept for most of the flight to London, curled up on a banquette with her head resting in Rafael's lap and her face pressed up against his waist while he worked on a laptop computer placed on the seat beside him. He was frowning in concentration, but was still aware of the way a set of her slender fingers had crept around his back and eased his shirt out of his trousers so she could have contact with his skin.

They were still making love. It had been like this for them from the first time he had dared to approach her with intimacy, days after they'd married. They'd been lying on a Caribbean beach, supposedly soaking up the sun, but the sensual vibrations flowing between them had reached such a pitch by then that it was either make a move or go back to their villa and take yet another long cold shower.

He had made the move, rolling onto his side, then over her. 'I want you,' he'd murmured, and kissed her before she'd had a chance to protest.

She hadn't protested, he recalled, giving up on trying to work and closing his eyes instead. They'd kissed themselves into a steamy stupor, then he'd gathered up enough sense to move location. He'd carried her back to the villa and she'd clung to him, blue eyes big and dark and driving him crazy—because they'd told him how much she wanted him.

A sigh threaded from him. Her cheek moved on his lap. It took some teeth-gritting control to stop his body from responding beneath that resting cheek.

They'd made love for the first time in the heat of the afternoon, and he'd never been so enchanted or so aware of his own prowess. She'd given him all of herself and he'd given the same back. He had never been the same man since. His cool English bride with her cool English reserve was not cool or reserved when it came to making love with him. And after the loving came this—the need to maintain contact with his skin, no matter where they were or how large the crowd they were in. She made him feel like the only man alive worthy of what she was giving him.

It had become like a drug. The more she'd made him feel the more he'd wanted her close—this close—all the time. When it had all exploded in his face it had been like having a vital part of him ripped out.

He'd become jealous and possessive, and moody with it. If he'd seen her look at another man and it had set his teeth on edge. She had worked for Daniel Fraser. They'd been an item before she'd arrived in Sicily to visit her grandfather. He'd heard about her—had known of her existence because Alessandro and Marisia talked about Louisa's half-English daughter who owned the big house on the hill.

Seeing her for the first time had been like being hit by a runaway truck. He had never expected to come up against love in any of its forms, never mind the kind that pinned him to the spot. He could not even say it was her fair-skinned beauty that had done it. He'd always preferred dark-haired women, who wore their desires on their warm golden faces, not blonde-haired blue-eyed creatures who wore their reserve like a wall of glass.

'What are you thinking about?' a sleepy voice murmured.

'You,' he replied.

'Thought so,' she said, and rubbed her cheek against his hardening shaft, before levering herself upward until her face came level with his. 'You have a one-track mind.'

'Mmm,' he agreed, waiting for the hand she had just removed from his back to find some other place to latch on. It found his nape, then clearly was not satisfied with that, and slid beneath the neck of his black tee shirt to curl into the tight satin muscle between his shoulder and neck.

Then she kissed him. It was a slow and sensual invitation, made all the more potent because they were hidden from view of everyone else by the bulkhead.

Did he want to make love here? All it would take

was a few strategic moves and she could be straddling him. She liked it like that. She liked to pin him down and ride him slowly. She liked having control of his hungry mouth. She was wearing a skirt, and his trouser zip was no real barrier. He could sit here and let her put him on another planet without having to do very much.

'You're thinking about it,' she murmured softly, reading his thoughts as if they belonged to her. 'Are you worried that we might get caught in the act?'

'No,' he said. 'And you are a tease.'

It was her turn to offer a sensuous little, 'Mmm.'

She kissed him again, holding his face between both hands now, and flexing her body with pleasure when his hands arrived at her waist. It was now or not at all, he told himself ruefully. She wanted him and he wanted her, so what was holding him back?

He frowned at the question. She sensed the frown and pulled back so she could look at him. 'I don't want to be a nuisance,' she drawled, ever so politely, and went to pull right back.

Which just about finished him.

His hand snaked up beneath her skirt and located her panties. He stripped them away without losing contact with her darkening, promising, beautiful eyes. Next he dealt with his fly zip, then picked her up and repositioned her across his lap.

The feel of him sliding into her dragged the air from her throat. She quivered, then settled on him for the few seconds it took for those first sensual tugs of her muscles to mould themselves around him. After that she rode him, slow and deep, his hands encasing her smooth behind, hers still framing his face. Eyes locked, breathing warm and heavy, she brought him to the edge.

'I love you,' she whispered, and tightened her muscles around him as he shattered, taking her with him as he did.

Afterwards she lay against him, shocked, he suspected, at what she'd encouraged them to do. 'You think I'm a hussy.' She confirmed his suspicions.

'I think you are amazingly, naturally generous, the way you give yourself to me.' He lifted a hand to her hair so he could use it to bring them face to face. 'I'm sorry I messed it up for us,' he said deeply. 'I mean to do better this time, I promise you.

'I just want you to love me,' she confided, and it was so vulnerable it made his heart clench.

'I do—believe me.' He kissed her gently, then added lightly, 'I am also fertile. Has it occurred to you yet that we have made love three times without using protection?'

Then, while she stared at him in shock at his revelation, he stood up with her still closed around him and made the few strides it took to take them to the tiny bathroom...

Christmas had already come to London. Festive lights hung across the streets and decorated shop windows.

Gino was driving them, with Parsons seated at his side and the usual glass partition separating the front of the car from the rear.

Nina sat quietly beside Rafael. She had not spoken much in the last hour and neither had he. She was still shocked by what he'd said to her on the plane—even more shocked at the casual way he had said it. Why he wasn't talking was less easy to explain.

She turned an anxious look on his smooth profile and instantly felt a warm feeling pool in the pit of her stomach. She had barely seen him as a living, breathing human being twelve short hours ago, and now he had become the very centre of her universe—again.

How had he managed to do that?

How had he turned this marriage of theirs around without seeming to do anything much at all other than argue a lot and—?

She tried shutting the next thought off before it got started, but she seemed to have lost the ability to do that. The walls had tumbled, leaving her open and exposed and feeling so very vulnerable that she wasn't at all certain she wanted to feel like this.

Warm and alive and fizzing with feeling. The champagne bubbles of earlier had nothing on what was circulating in her blood right now.

Awareness—sexual awareness—spiced up with words of love…

He still had her panties. He'd refused to give them back to her, and now here she was, fizzing away in the knowledge that she was sitting here primly beside him with no underwear on because it was stuffed in his jacket pocket.

And could you tell that from that smooth, lean, too-handsome-to-be-true profile? No, you could not. The chin was level, the mouth flat, there wasn't a hair out of place on his dark silk head or a single crease in his dark suit that might hint he had been doing anything other than travelling from A to B in the trouble-free ease with which sophisticated and wealthy businessmen expected to travel.

Rafael had walls of his own that kept people out when he wanted it that way. He'd allowed her a glimpse of the vulnerable man earlier, the needy man—both emotionally and physically—the man with weaknesses and fears like everyone else. But he'd let her see that man once before, only to slam the walls up when she'd dared to step too far over the line.

Where was the line going to be this time? Where were they about to go from here? How could he be so calm about them having unprotected sex when only six months ago the very idea that he could be sowing fertile seed had horrified him?

'You're sure you don't mind about—?'

'Yes,' he responded. That was all. After hours of silence between them he'd anticipated what she had been about to ask him and given his answer, neat and precise.

Nina pressed her lips together and looked to the front again. What was that reply supposed to represent? Don't speak about it because I might change my mind? Or why bother to ask when the deed has been done?

A fatalist. Was he a fatalist? Was she being a complete fool to let him close again when he'd proved time after time that he could let her down badly when she needed him most?

The car turned into one of those streets that made Mayfair the exclusive district it was. As Gino guided it into its reserved off-road parking space Nina looked up at the elegant building which housed elegant apartments for elegant people.

Her father had used to own an apartment like this. Her mother had it now, left to her as her only bequest from Richard St James, along with a cold comment: The only part of my life that gave my wife pleasure. He'd been referring to the apartment's position within the high society life Louisa loved to live. Her father had been a cold man, and very bitter by the end. He'd loved Nina in a fashion—but not enough to let her warm his heart.

Rafael was like that. A man whose needs were tempered by the amount of feeling he was prepared to give out.

The car engine went silent. Parsons got out and opened Nina's door for her. Nobody spoke as all four of them walked towards the glass doors through which Louisa had spied Rafael and Marisia waiting for the lift to come.

Marisia… A sudden cold little draft feathered Nina's skin. They still had not finished with the Marisia thing, and Rafael *had* brought her here, and they *had* stood together in this very foyer, touching and gazing at each other intimately.

The lift was there waiting for them, instead of the other way round, so they rode it together—the man and his wife, the butler and the chauffeur-cum-bodyguard.

An odd bunch, Nina thought wryly.

Beside her, Rafael shifted his stance and she glanced up, met with a pair of half-hidden glinting black eyes. He wasn't hiding, he was waiting, she realised. Biding his time until he got her alone and begin the whole sensual experience all over again.

Had he ridden in this lift wearing the same look for Marisia?

Stop it, she told herself crossly. This is just being silly.

But even as they emptied out of the lift tension was be-

ginning to creep up her spine. What if she found something inside the apartment—proof that there had been
more to Rafael and Marisia's night together than
just—?

His hand came to rest at the base of her spine as they
waited for Gino to use his key to open the apartment
door. Maybe he could feel her tension, because she felt
his fingers begin to knead.

It was better to move away—easy to do it when she
could follow Gino through the door.

'Go and get some sleep,' Rafael told Parsons and
Gino as soon as they were all inside.

'You don't want me to make something warm to
drink before I—?'

'No—thank you,' he murmured politely to the butler.
'*Grazie,* Gino.'

The chauffeur was wiser than Parsons. He knew
when they were not wanted. With a nod he ushered the
butler towards the back of the apartment, where their
private rooms were situated.

And then they were alone.

'Shall we do the same?' he invited softly, and Nina
jerked into movement, walking forward down the
spacious hallway, bypassing the elegant reception
rooms on either side of her and only pausing when she
found herself standing in the centre of the bedroom
they'd used to share.

Removing her coat as she looked around her, she was
aware of Rafael standing in the doorway, watching her
familiarise herself with the straw-coloured walls, the
dark furniture and the soft furnishings in subtle shades
of copper and bronze.

She was looking for signs of female occupation. She knew it; he knew it.

'Found anything?' he asked.

She made no answer. Instead she dropped her coat across the back of one of the soft-cushioned chairs that flanked the white marble fireplace, then turned to head for the connecting bathroom.

'Don't try it, *cara*,' his smooth voice advised her. 'If something is bothering you then say so, but do not walk away.'

'All right.' She spun round to face him.

He was propping up the doorway with a broad shoulder, arms casually folded across his chest and everything about him as relaxed as a man could get. But it was all just a front, because there was nothing relaxed about his narrow-eyed, flat-lipped expression. He was ready for this.

'Where did she sleep?' she demanded.

'In the small guest room at the end of the hall,' he supplied.

'No diversions along the way?' she challenged. 'No deep and meaningful talks over a pot of coffee followed by some comforting hugs and kisses to reassure her? You just marched her down the hall to the small guest room and shut her inside it, then shut yourself in here?'

'You asked me where she slept, not what came beforehand,' he answered smoothly. 'I've told you nothing happened. Why are you fixating on this?'

'Because I have an issue about the two of you maintaining contact throughout our marriage,' she said. 'It's all a bit too cosy, very clandestine—and if I catch a whiff of her scent in any corner of this suite I will never believe another word you say to me!'

With that she turned towards the bathroom.

'She did not come in here.'

'Good,' she said, and kept on going.

'And what you call being clandestine I call being sensitive to your feelings and sympathetic to hers. I all but dumped her for you—does that count for nothing?'

'No,' she replied. 'It sounds like one big cover-up to me.'

'Cover-up of what?'

Nina twisted back. He still hadn't moved from the door, but his arms had unfolded and now he was angry. 'A few nights ago you had another woman sleeping in this apartment.' She spelled it out for him. 'Twelve hours ago our marriage was nothing but a very bad joke. Since then I've been humiliated in front of my family, thoroughly seduced by you, and uprooted from Sicily and replanted here. My panties now reside in one of your pockets, like some kind of trophy—'

'Due to your seduction of me,' he put in.

Cheeks flushing, she ignored that. 'You've been leading me around by the nose and I don't know why I'm letting you do it!'

'Because you want to?'

'Oh!' she exclaimed, because he was so right. She almost stamped her foot in angry frustration. She retreated to the bathroom instead.

When she came out again, wearing one of the soft bathrobes that always hung behind the door, she found him waiting for her—dangling her flimsy white lace panties from his fingers like a taunt.

'I kept these,' he said, 'because you knowing I had them added an excruciating kind of tension to the rest of our journey. And I wanted to keep us both up there on a sexual high until I could get you alone.'

Nina snatched them away from him, so full of tumbling conflictions she didn't know whether to laugh at his audacity or just break down and cry.

'A few days ago you were still the only woman I wanted near me,' he continued. 'Twelve hours ago our marriage was in a mess, but salvageable—thank God. I had no wish to humiliate you and I did not seduce you. We made love,' he declared, 'because we both badly needed to, and I uprooted you from Sicily to offset a fight with your grandfather until he learns the truth, and because you were in danger of being swallowed up by that cold, empty shell of a house!'

Her sharp gasp at that last part had him muttering something, but did not stop him from going on. 'Marisia is not and never has been my lover. I did not break any code of marital ethics by bringing her to stay here for the night.'

'So if I brought Fredo to stay here overnight you would have no problem with it? Is that what you're saying?'

'No I am not saying that.' His mouth snapped together and he frowned.

'Then stop expecting more of me than you can give back,' she denounced. 'Now, I'm tired, so I'm going to bed—to sleep,' she added as a warning afterthought.

With that she stalked around him, walked up to the huge, deeply sprung divan bed, dropped her robe to the carpet like a defiance, then lifted a corner of the featherlight duvet and slipped between it and the cool cotton sheet.

If she'd expected a response then she did not get one. As she lay there shivering—the bed was cold and she was wearing nothing because her hastily packed suitcase still languished in the boot of the car—that other part of her—the part trembling with expectancy— withered when she heard the bathroom door quietly close.

He was taking his turn in the bathroom. Nina curled onto her side, closed her eyes, and grimly willed herself to fall asleep before he returned.

Surprisingly, it happened. One second she was deciding how she was going to freeze him out when he joined her in the bed, and the next moment she'd simply dropped like a stone into a deep sleep.

CHAPTER TEN

BY THE time Rafael approached the bed she was so
deeply asleep that he found himself smiling ruefully as
he slid in beside her. With a stealth aimed not to awaken
her he drew her naked body into the curve of his, whispered, 'Shh,' when she murmured something, then
reached out to touch a switch by the bed, plunging the
room into darkness. Then he settled his head on the
pillow beside her, closed his eyes, and at last dared to
let himself relax.

Two hours later a grey winter dawn seeped slowly
into the bedroom. Two hours after that neither of them
had moved. Two hours on again the familiar feel of his
hand gently stroking between her thighs plus the wet
heat of his mouth tugging gently on one of her breasts
brought her awake.

She opened her eyes to find harsh daylight softened
by the curtains still drawn across the window. She was
still for a few seconds, absorbing the sultry hush that
lay over everything. Then blue eyes drifted down to
where his head covered her breast. Dark hair tumbled
like springy silk, and tanned shoulders were glossed by

those natural oils which came during sleep to lubricate skin like stretched leather.

Lifting a hand, she let her fingers gently trail through his hair, making him raise his head, lips still parted and moist, eyes dark with desire as they clashed with hers.

'*Ciao,*' he greeted softly.

'*Ciao.*' She smiled.

The smile had its effect. 'You still love me,' he declared.

Why deny it? Nina thought. So, 'Yes,' she sighed, and received her reward in the warm crush of his mouth on hers.

Making love with Rafael in the morning had always been special. Nina thought it had something to do with him not yet having had the chance to pull on his sophisticated garb, so she got the real man—raw passions and all.

He liked to watch her melt; he liked to make her cling to him and plead and beg in a breathlessly sensuous voice. And when he came inside her he liked to make sure every inch of flesh possible enjoyed the experience at the same time. Arms wrapped around her and long legs tangled with hers, their bodies in touch from breast to hip and their mouths bonded as if they would never be able to break them apart.

He was everything her heart desired when he was like this—giving yet demanding, darkly passionate yet unbelievably willing to let her know how deeply she affected him.

At some point while he was stroking them towards the waiting turbulent climax the doorbell rang. If either heard it they dismissed it, because what was happening here was so much more important than anything else.

The first ripples of release began to shake her body,

and his tongue caught her gasps of pleasure as he increased his stroke. Slow and deep, harder with each thrust. She clung with her hands to his neck and his back—to his solid calf muscles with the bare soles of her feet and curling toes. Then came the blinding rush of orgasm, the tight, tingling shots of electric pleasure, which flowed between them in the kind of fusing that turned two into a whole.

It was no use trying to move afterwards. No part of either of them was fit to move. He was heavy on her, yet she felt as if she was floating, and she never wanted to come down to earth again.

A light rap on the bedroom door warned of Parsons's imminent arrival. With a muttered curse Rafael responded like lightning, by reaching out with a hand to grab hold of the duvet. The next thing Nina knew they were buried beneath it, and Rafael was still cursing as he covered her shocked face with kisses.

The door opened. A short silence prevailed. Nina felt the nervous urge to giggle, but that urge quickly died when the butler announced, 'Mrs St James and Miss Marisia have arrived and are asking to see you, sir—madam…'

The door closed again. Another short silence arrived. Then Rafael was pushing back the all-enveloping duvet and launching himself off the bed. Nina shivered at the loss—not of the duvet but the man.

'Stay here,' he instructed angrily. 'I will deal with this.'

'Not this time.' Nina was off the bed and stooping to pick up the bathrobe from the floor. 'If Marisia is here to cause trouble then she will do it to my face.'

He paused on his way to the wardrobes, turned to utter a protest, then saw the stubborn look on her face.

'You're going out there looking like that?' he asked as he watched her cinch the robe's belt around her waist.

'Why not?' Her chin came up, her face still wearing the flush of loving but her eyes like blue glass again. 'Does it bother you that she will guess what we've been doing in here?'

'*Dio,*' he rasped. 'You still don't believe me about her!'

'You should not have brought her to this apartment,' she said, turning away from the sheer beauty of this naked man, still aroused and angry with it.

'If you wish to play it this way then so be it,' he said, and diverted from the wardrobes to the bathroom. A second later he was pulling on a matching bathrobe and striding across the room in the other direction, to open the bedroom door.

His mocking bow invited her to precede him. Nina sailed past him with her chin in the air—only to find herself captured by a strong arm that curved her into his body.

'One day,' he murmured, 'you are going to have to concede you are wrong about me, and when that day comes I will expect a full apology—on my own very particular terms.' Then he swept the two of them down the hall and into the sitting room.

The first thing to hit Nina was the delicious smell of freshly made coffee; the next was the sight of her mother, standing staring out of the window, holding a cup and saucer in her hand. Louisa was wearing black today. Black wool suit and black silk shirt that looked very dramatic against the tense paleness showing on her face as she turned to look at them.

Marisia was sitting in one of the soft leather easy

chairs. She was wearing black too, and also looked pale. She managed a brief glance upwards, then flushed and quickly looked down again.

'This is an unexpected surprise,' Rafael said lightly as he drew Nina forward. 'The two of you must have been up with the birds to get here so early.'

'We are sorry to have disturbed you,' Louisa responded, with a contemptuous glance at the way they were dressed. 'But it is one-thirty in the afternoon.'

'So late?' he quizzed. 'We had not noticed. Did Gino frisk you for lethal weapons, by the way?'

The taunt went home like its own lethal weapon. Louisa suddenly looked uncomfortable, and Marisia shot upright, seeming to only just notice their hastily donned bathrobes, dishevelled hair and bare feet. She blanched, then sent a pained, pale and pleading look towards Rafael.

'We have intruded. I apologise,' she said anxiously. 'We should not have come—'

'Speak for yourself, Marisia,' Louisa said coolly. 'And sit down again, before you fall down.'

It was a surprise to watch Marisia do exactly that, but it was the way she put a trembling hand to her lips that struck a chord in Nina that sent her forward to squat down in front of her cousin.

'You're feeling unwell, aren't you?' she said, recognising the signs, having experienced them for herself.

'It was the sudden movement.' Marisia wafted a hand over her mouth, then tried swallowing. 'I will be all right in moment. I just need—'

'To wait for the nausea to recede. I know,' Nina put in. 'Can we get you anything? A glass of water? Or would you like to lie down or—?'

'Oh, please don't be nice to me, Nina!' Marisia protested painfully. 'I did a terrible thing to you last night. I forgot about the baby you lost when I spoke out as I did. Rafael told me not to do it, but I thought—'

'She thought she would be saved from my father's wrath with all of us there,' Louisa finished for her. 'And ended up causing more trouble than she is actually worth—did you not, *cara*?'

'You are a hard woman, Zia Louisa!' Marisia cried.

'If your mother was alive you would be confined to your room by now and not allowed to leave again for the next seven months!'

'What do you know about being a mother?' Nina snapped, shocking everyone by coming down on her cousin's side. 'You were never there for me!'

'Well, I am here now,' Louisa said, completely unfazed by the criticism. 'Tell Nina the name of the man whose baby it is you are carrying, and let us get this over with.'

Rafael stiffened in readiness. Nina's heart lodged like a brick in her throat.

Marisia swallowed thickly, 'H-his name is not important,' she said. 'But I can tell you it is not Rafael.'

Nina sat back on her haunches. 'But you said—'

'I offered no name,' Marisia insisted.

'No.' Louisa sighed suddenly. 'I am afraid, *cara*, that was me.'

Bewildered, Nina stared from one face to the other. 'I'm not following this…'

'Then let me explain,' her mother said, and came to put down her cup and saucer, then released another sigh and sat down herself.

'You know I had seen them being very intense over

a dinner table,' she reminded Nina. 'You also know that I followed them back here, and what I saw then.'

Rafael made himself comfortable on the arm of a chair and waited with interest for this to play itself out.

'When Marisia said what she did last night I put two and two together and came up with—Rafael. You ran from the room and I wanted to kill someone. Rafael went after you and I told everyone that he was the father of Marisia's child.'

'I should have corrected her,' Marisia put in. 'But everyone was so busy shouting at each other that they seemed to have forgotten I was there, and I—preferred to keep it that way.'

'Lovely child,' Louisa derided her twin sister's daughter. 'What she means is that she took the coward's way out and let Rafael take the heat.'

'I did not think that Nonno would chase off to kill Rafael!' Marisia said defensively. 'We are supposed to live in the twenty-first century, for goodness' sake!'

'He was defending your honour.'

'He was defending Nina's honour,' Marisia threw back. 'He's always preferred her to me—'

'No, he hasn't,' Nina denied. 'He adores you. You are his beautiful dark-haired princess while I am—'

'His golden-haired angel sent from heaven for him to cherish…'

The two cousins looked at each other, then actually laughed—because it was so typical of him to play one off against the other.

'Glad you find all of this amusing, but I am still the man on his hit list,' Rafael put in.

The three women turned to look at him, their expressions telling him that they'd completely forgotten he was even there.

'My apologies,' he mocked, 'for butting in with my problems.'

Then he sent Nina the kind of smile that told her how much he was going to enjoy his apology later.

She looked away quickly, her cheeks growing warm. 'I hope you haven't come to London without telling Nonno the truth,' she said sharply.

'Of course not,' her mother snapped. 'To give Marisia her due, she told the truth as soon as the lynch mob arrived back without Rafael's head on a stick.'

'Better late than too late, I suppose,' Rafael murmured dryly.

'If I thought that you could not hold your own against a seventy-year-old man and his two middle-aged sons I would say you were not worth saving,' his mother-in-law said. 'And don't think that because I was wrong about what I saw that I have forgiven you for the way you have been neglecting my daughter when she needed—'

'All right—let's not start another war,' Nina cut in quickly. 'I told you yesterday, Mother, that my marriage is none of your business.'

'*Grazie, cara,*' Rafael said.

'I did not mean to imply that what she said was wrong!' she flashed at him.

'You have come alive again,' Louisa observed.

'I was not dead, just grieving.' Nina came to her feet. 'How is Nonno feeling now that he knows the truth?' She brought this discussion firmly back on track.

'Devastated,' Louisa said. 'He has convinced himself that he has forfeited your love.'

'But that's silly.' Nina frowned.

'Tell *him* that, not me. You left Sicily, darling. He has translated that into you leaving him.'

'Rafael...' Nina spun anxiously to look at him. 'I don't want him to feel...'

He had straightened and taken her in his arms before she had a chance to finish the sentence. 'We can deal with him later,' he assured her, then a pair of warm lips brushed hers, and for a few glistening seconds Nina was not in the room.

'Time for us to go, I think,' Louisa said dryly, getting to her feet. Then she turned a wary look on her daughter. 'I hope you don't mind, Nina, but Marisia is coming to live with me here in London for a while—until she decides what it is she wants to do.'

'With the baby?' Nina turned her anxious look on her cousin next.

'No,' Marisia said, and the way her hands spread a protective cover over her abdomen said everything that needed to be said. 'You were right, Rafael.' She glanced at him. 'I have learned to love this baby. I just needed the extra time to realise it. I will bring it up alone, no matter what my family think or what sacrifices I will have to make.'

'My offer still stands,' he told her quietly.

What offer? Nina frowned at him. He ignored her questioning frown.

'Thank you,' Marisia murmured. 'I will keep it in mind.'

'What offer did you make to her?' Nina demanded the moment they were alone again.

'Marisia has discovered that she has a gift for picking

out photogenic faces, so I offered to set her up with her own agency,' he explained.

'Right here in London?'

'Or Paris—Milan.' He shrugged.

'Make it Milan,' Nina said decisively. 'It isn't a city you visit that much.'

'You really are a jealous witch,' he drawled lazily.

'She's still in love with you—and don't tell me I don't know what I'm talking about,' she warned when he opened his mouth to speak. 'Even sitting in that chair, feeling sick and worried for herself, she still had to keep throwing those coded glances at you!'

He laughed. It was infuriating.

The next thing she knew she was being scooped off her feet. A minute later she was naked and back in the tumbled bed, with an equally naked Rafael on top of her. What followed next was his idea of how she should apologise for not believing him...

Later—much later—he was in a lazy, playful mood, pressing light kisses in rows across the flat of her abdomen, 'What do you think?' he said. 'Have we managed to make a baby yet, or do we need to try again?'

'I don't understand why you've changed you mind about children.' Nina frowned. 'I don't mind, you know, if the idea really upsets you. I only needed you to explain it to me before I got pregnant. Not—'

'Cruelly and heartlessly afterwards.'

'You were punishing me because you thought the baby wasn't yours.'

'You are very charitable, *cara*, but I don't need excuses made for me. I was a—bastard to you.' That was the first time he had ever used the word, and it surprised him as much as it did Nina to hear it fall from his lips. He slid up the bed to come and lie beside her. 'I will make it up to you,' he vowed huskily.

He was referring to the lost baby, Nina knew that, but...

She turned to face him on the pillow. 'Do you love me, Rafael?'

'More than I can deal with sometimes,' he admitted, and touched her cheek with a tenderness that almost brought tears.

'You know I love you the same way, so we don't need—'

'No.' The fingers on her cheek moved to cover her mouth. 'It's you who does not understand, *amore*, that I wanted the baby to be mine so badly that every one of my foolish objections just paled into insignificance on the strength of that need. I've grown up, Nina. I've shed my past. I will never know who my parents are, but that's OK. Our children *will* know their parents. They will be loved and cared for and protected, and they will grow into good, strong people because that is what we will teach them to be. And,' he added on a lighter note, aimed to lift the serious mood, 'finding out I have a very healthy sperm count has placed a spectacular new edge on making love with you. Kind of—lusty and macho,' he said, with a lusty groan as he tipped her onto her back so he could lean over her.

'Oh, no, you don't,' she said, pushing him away. 'I'm hungry and thirsty. Have you any idea when we last ate anything? Because I haven't. And I have to call Nonno,' she reminded him.

'Do you want to go back?' he asked.

'To Sicily? No.' She snuggled into to him. 'I'm happy right where I am.'

'Then go and call him up—invite him for Christmas. Hell, invite them all if you want!' he said. 'If it makes him feel better about coming then I will even go against my better instincts and finance his latest disaster for him!'

A knock sounded at the bedroom door.

Parsons did not let himself in this time, but waited for Nina to scramble off the bed and pull on a bathrobe before she opened it. 'Your grandfather has arrived,' he informed her. 'Gino has checked him out and he seems—safe. What would you like us to do with him?'

Nina turned to look at Rafael. 'Oh, dear,' she said solemnly.

Oh, dear just about said it, Rafael thought as he made a reluctant shift from the bed. One old man with his dignity in tatters was going to take a lot of soothing.

'This is going to cost me,' he muttered ruefully.

'You can afford it,' his wife said. 'Just think about the payback when I show you my gratitude and you will be fine…'

There are 24 timeless classics in the Mills & Boon® 100th Birthday Collection

Two of these beautiful stories are out each month. Make sure you collect them all!

If you have missed any of these books, log on to www.millsandboon.co.uk to order your copies online.